se for *The Old Gringo*

A challenging meditation on politics, love and the burden of history itself . . . What lingers most in this profound work are the images that convey the wondrous grandeur of a society in transformation. *The Old Gringo* is a brilliant fiction, a luminous and compelling chronicle.

—Henry Mayer, *San Francisco Chronicle*

Sensual and mind-pleasing . . . *The Old Gringo* . . . is the work of an integrated personality, the artist who contains and illuminates all the layers of all the times and cultures of a nation.

—Earl Shorris, *The New York Times Book Review*

Fuentes gives us history as a dream that we might knowingly inhabit, where, as in a dream, the most extraordinary events would require no explanation.

—Jay Cantor, *The Boston Globe*

In *The Old Gringo* Carlos Fuentes levels his gaze on a triad of weighty subjects: the Mexican Revolution, a still-innocent United States and the enigmatic career of its most curious man of letters. That he illuminates all three in a slim volume is a tribute to the economical power of his art. It radiates authenticity. Fuentes understands the Mexican Revolution as only a visionary can.

—Dennis Drabelle, *USA Today*

D0954192

ALSO BY CARLOS FUENTES

THE OLD GRINGO

THE OLD GRINGO

by

CARLOS FUENTES

Translated from the Spanish by

MARGARET SAYERS PEDEN

and the author

Farrar   Straus   Giroux
New York

Farrar, Straus and Giroux
18 West 18th Street, New York 10011

Library of Congress Control Number: 2006938245
Paperback ISBN-13: 978-0-374-53052-5
Paperback ISBN-10: 0-374-53052-1

Designed by Claudia Carlson

www.fsgbooks.com

7   9   10   8

To William Styron
whose father included me in
his dreams of the American Civil War

But who knows the fate of his bones
or how often he is to be buried?
                              Sir Thomas Browne

What they call dying
is merely the last pain.
                              Ambrose Bierce

THE OLD GRINGO

1 Now she sits alone and remembers.

She sees, over and over, the specters of Tomás Arroyo and the moon-faced woman and the old gringo cross her window. But they are not ghosts. They have simply mobilized their old pasts, hoping that she would do the same and join them.

But for her it took a long time.

First, she had to stop hating Tomás Arroyo for showing her what she could be and then forbidding her to ever be what she might be.

And he knew that she could never be that, and in spite of knowing it, he let her see it.

He always knew that she would return home.

But he let her see what would become of her if she remained.

She had to purge herself of this hatred. It took her many years to do so. The old gringo was no longer there to help her. Arroyo was not there. Tom Brook. He might have given her a child by that name. She had no right to think this. The moon-faced woman had taken him with her toward their nameless destiny. Tomás Arroyo was over.

So the only moment she had left was when she crossed the border and looked back at the two men, the soldier Inocencio and the boy Pedrito. Behind them, she now thought she saw the dust marshaling itself into some kind of silent chronology that told her to remember;

she had come back to her land without memory, and Mexico was no longer available, Mexico had disappeared forever, but across that bridge, on the other side of the river, a memorious dust insisted on marshaling itself for her, on crossing the frontier and sweeping over the shrub and the wheat fields, the plains and the smoky mountains, the long deep green rivers that the old man had pined for, right up to her walk-up apartment in Washington, D.C., on the shores of the Potomac, the Atlantic, the center of the world.

The dust blew and told her that she was alone.

She remembers.

Alone.

2 "The old gringo came to Mexico to die."

Colonel Frutos García ordered the lanterns placed in a circle around the mound. Sweating soldiers, naked to the waist, with sweaty necks, grabbed their shovels and began to dig in earnest, driving their spades into the mesquite.

Old gringo: that's what they called the man the Colonel was remembering now as young Pedro followed every move of the men laboring in the desert night; again, the boy saw a bullet piercing a silver peso in midair.

"It was pure chance that we met that morning in Chihuahua. He never told us, but we all knew why he'd come. He wanted us to kill him, us Mexicans. That's why he was here. That's why he'd crossed the frontier, back in the days when very few of us ever left the place where we were born."

[4]

The spadefuls of dirt were like red clouds strayed from the sky: too low, too near the lantern light. *They* did, said Colonel García, yes, the gringos did. They spent their lives crossing frontiers, theirs and those that belonged to others, and now the old man had crossed to the south because he didn't have any frontiers left to cross in his own country.

"Easy there."

"And the frontier in here?" the North American woman had asked, tapping her forehead. "And the frontier in here?" General Arroyo had responded, touching his heart. "There's one frontier we only dare to cross at night," the old gringo said. "The frontier of our differences with others, of our battles with ourselves."

"The old gringo died in Mexico. And all because he crossed the frontier. Wasn't that reason enough?" asked Colonel Frutos García.

"Do you remember how he trembled if he cut his face shaving?" asked Inocencio Mansalvo, his narrow green eyes no more than slits.

"Or how afraid he was of mad dogs?" added the Colonel.

"That isn't true," said young Pedro. "He was brave."

"Well, I always thought he was a saint," said La Garduña, laughing.

"No, all he ever wanted was to be always remembered as he was," said Harriet Winslow.

"Easy, easy there."

"Much later, when little by little we were able to piece together the bits of his life, we understood why the old gringo had come to Mexico. He did the right thing, I suppose. As soon as he came, he let everyone know he was tired, that things just weren't the same anymore, but we respected him because we never saw him tired here, and he proved himself as brave as any man. You're right, boy. Too brave for his own good."

"Easy."

The spades struck wood and the soldiers paused for a minute, wiping the sweat from their foreheads.

The old gringo used to joke: "I want to go see if those Mexicans can shoot straight. My work is finished, and so am I." I like the game, he'd said, I like the fighting; I want to see it.

"Yes sir, you could see 'farewell' in his eyes."

"He didn't have any family."

"He retired and then wandered through the lands of his youth—California, where he'd worked as a journalist; the southern United States, where he'd fought during the Civil War; New Orleans, where he liked to drink and womanize and feel he was the devil himself."

"Ah, our know-it-all colonel."

"Watch it with our colonel; he makes you think he's dead drunk but he's really listening."

"And now Mexico: a family memory. His father had been here, too, as a soldier, when they invaded us more than a half century ago."

"He was a soldier, he fought against naked savages and followed his country's flag to the capital of a civilized race far to the south."

The old gringo joked: I want to see whether those Mexicans can shoot straight. "My work is finished, and so am I."

"This is something we didn't understand because what we saw was an erect old man, stiff as a ramrod, with hands steady as a rock. Yes, if he joined General Arroyo's troops it was because you yourself, Pedrito, gave him the chance and he earned it with a Colt .44."

The men knelt around the open grave and scrabbled at the corners of the pine box.

"But he also said that to be stood up against a Mexican stone wall and shot to rags was a pretty good way to depart this life. He used to smile and say: 'It beats old age, disease, or falling down the cellar stairs.' "

The Colonel was silent for a moment: he had the distinct impression that he'd heard a raindrop falling in the middle of the desert. He looked at the clear sky. The ocean sound faded away.

"We never knew his real name," he added, looking at Inocencio Mansalvo, half naked and sweating, on his knees before the heavy coffin tenaciously clinging to the desert, as if in such a short time it had taken root. "We have trouble with gringo names, just like gringo faces, they all look alike; their language sounds like Chinese."

La Garduña, who wouldn't miss a burial for anything in this world, to say nothing of an exhumation, bellowed her laughter. "Their blurred faces are Chinese to us, all exactly alike."

Inocencio Mansalvo ripped a half-rotten plank from the coffin and they saw the face of the old gringo, devoured more by night than by death: devoured, thought Colonel Frutos García, by nature. The weather-beaten, greenish face was strangely smiling; the rictus of death exposed gums and long teeth—the teeth of a gringo or a horse—forming an eternally sardonic grimace.

Everyone stood for a minute looking at what the night lights revealed, the twin lights of the sunken but open eyes of the corpse. What caught the boy's attention was that the gringo's hair, in death, seemed neatly combed, every white strand in place, as if down there a tiny devil in charge of hair were responsible for a trim that would look as neat as a new-mown field when dead men found themselves face to face with the Grim Reaper.

"Grim Reaper!" guffawed the woman called La Garduña.

"Hurry it up, hurry now," ordered Frutos García. "Let's get him out of there. By tomorrow morning early, we're supposed to have the old bastard in Camargo." His voice was strained. "Hurry now; we have a long dusty road ahead of us, and if a wind comes up, the old gringo'll be gone forever . . ."

The truth is, it almost happened that way, wind blowing across saline, boggy wasteland, this land of unconquered Indians and renegade Spanish, bold cattle rustlers and mines abandoned to the dark floods of hell. The truth is, the corpse of the old gringo almost faded into the desert wind, as if the frontier he had crossed one day had been air, not earth, and had encompassed all the times everyone could remember, suspended there, with an exhumed body in their arms: La Garduña brushing the dirt from the old gringo's body, moaning, hurrying; the boy, not daring to touch the dead man; the others blindly remembering the long spans and vast spaces on both sides of the wound that to the north opened like the Rio Grande itself rushing down from steep canyons, as far up as the Sangre de Cristo Mountains, islands in the deserts of the north, ancient lands of the Pueblos, the Navajos and Apaches, hunters and peasants only half subdued by Spain's adventures in the New World, they, from the lands of Chihuahua and the Rio Grande, both seemed to die here, on this high plain where a group of soldiers for a few seconds held the pose of the Pietà, dazed by what they'd done and by an accompanying compassion, until the Colonel broke the spell: Hurry, boys, we have to get the gringo back to his own country; those are our General's orders.

And then he saw the sunken blue eyes of the dead man and he was afraid, because for an instant they lacked the distance men want death to have. And because they seemed still alive, he spoke to those eyes: "Haven't you ever thought, you gringos, that all this land was once ours? Ah, our resentment and our memory go hand in hand."

Inocencio Mansalvo stared at his colonel and put on his dirt-covered Stetson. He walked to his horse, spraying dirt from his hat, and then everything speeded up, actions, orders, movements: a single scene, farther and farther in the distance, fading until the group receded from view: Colonel Frutos García and young Pedro, the guffawing Garduña and the exhausted Inocencio Mansalvo, the soldiers and the rigid corpse of the old gringo wrapped in a blanket and strapped to the sled of the desert, a litter of ocote and leather thongs, dragged by two blindfolded horses.

" 'To be a gringo in Mexico.' " The Colonel smiled. " 'Ah, that is euthanasia.' That's what the old gringo said."

3

As soon as he crossed the Rio Grande, he heard the explosion and turned to see the bridge in flames.

He got off the train in El Paso, carrying his folding black suitcase, what they called a Gladstone then, and dressed all in black except for the white expanse of cuffs and shirtfront. He'd told himself he wasn't going to need much luggage on this trip. He walked a few blocks through the border town; he'd imagined it drearier and duller and older than it actually was, and sick, as well, of the Revolution, of the rage from across the river. Instead, it was a town of bright new automobiles, five-and-ten-cent stores, and young people, so young they could hardly have been born in the nineteenth century. In vain, he searched for his idea of the American frontier. It wasn't going to be easy to buy a horse without having to fend off inopportune questions about the horseman's destination.

He could cross the frontier and buy a horse in Mexico. But the old man wanted to make life difficult for himself. Besides, he'd got it in his head that he needed an American horse. If they opened his suitcase at customs, all they'd find would be a few ham sandwiches, a safety razor, a toothbrush, a couple of his own books, a copy of *Don Quixote*, a clean shirt, and a Colt .44 wrapped in his underclothes. He didn't want to explain why he was traveling with such a light, if precise, array of provisions.

"I intend to be a good-looking corpse."

"And the books, señor?"

"They're mine."

"No one suggested you'd stolen them."

Resigned, the old man would offer no further explanations. "All my life I've wanted to read the *Quixote*. I'd like to do it before I die. I've given up writing forever."

He imagined this scene, and told the man who sold him the horse that he was going to look north of the city for land to develop; a horse was still more useful in the sagebrush than one of those infernal machines. The dealer said that was true; he wished everyone thought like him, because no one was buying horses these days except agents for the Mexican rebels. But that's why the price was a little steep; there was a revolution on the other side of the border, and revolutions are good for business.

"Yes, there's still a place for a good horse," said the old man, and rode off on a white mare that would be visible at night and would make life difficult for her owner when he wanted his life to be difficult.

Now he had to keep his sense of direction, because although the frontier was traced broad and clear by the river dividing El Paso from Ciudad Juárez, beyond the Mexican town there was no demarcation but the line in the distance where sky joined dry, dirty plain.

That horizon kept receding as the old man rode on, his long legs dangling beneath the mare's belly, his black suitcase cradled in his lap. Some twenty kilometers west of El Paso, he forded the river at its narrowest point while everyone's attention was diverted by the explosion on the bridge. At that instant, in the old man's clear eyes were fused all the cities of gold, the expeditions that never returned, the lost priests, the nomadic and moribund tribes of Tobosos and Laguneros that had survived the epidemics of the Europeans and then fled the Spanish towns to master the horse, the bow, and later the rifle, in an endless ebb and flow of beginnings and dissolutions, mining bonanzas and depression, genocides as vast as the land itself and as forgotten as the accumulated bitterness of its men.

Rebellion and suppression, plague and famine—the old man knew he was entering the restless lands of Chihuahua and the Rio Grande, leaving behind the refuge of El Paso, founded with a hundred and thirty settlers and seven thousand head of cattle. He was abandoning the sacred refuge of fugitives from the north and from the south: a flimsy, precarious haven in harsh desert lands: one main street, a hotel and a pianola, soda fountains and hiccuping Fords, and the answer of the invading north to the mirages of the desert: an iron suspension bridge, a railroad station, a blue haze imported from Chicago and Philadelphia.

He himself was now a voluntary fugitive, as much a fugitive as the ancient survivors of the attacks of Conchos and Apaches whom cruel necessity, sickness, injustice, and disillusion had once again driven to wandering: all this was etched in the old gringo's head as he crossed the frontier between Mexico and the United States. No wonder they had all tired of continual flight and for over a hundred years remained entangled in the thorns of the hacienda system.

But maybe he was carrying a different fear, one he voiced as he crossed the frontier: "I'm afraid that each of us carries the real frontier inside."

The bridge exploded in the distance and he headed to the right and to the south, feeling sure of his bearings (he was already in Mexico, that was enough) when about dusk he smelled warm tortillas and beans.

[12]

He approached the small gray adobe hut and asked, in his accented Spanish, whether they could offer him a meal and a blanket to sleep on. The fat owners of the smoky house said yes, *ésta es su casa, señor.*

He knew the ritual phrase of Mexican courtesy but suspected that after having offered him the house, his host would feel free to subject his guest to all manner of whims and insults, especially any arising from jealous suspicion. But he curbed his desire to stir up a fight; not yet, he told himself, not yet. That night, drowsing on the straw mat in his black clothes, listening to the heavy breathing of his hosts and their dogs, smelling the heavy odors of the couple, different from his because they ate differently and thought and loved and feared differently, it pleased him that they'd offered him their house. What had he lost, in four successive and irreparable blows, but that? In the end, what other reason had he, he admitted, countering his own sleepy but malicious wink, for trotting off toward the south, the only frontier left to him after exhausting in his seventy-one years the other three boundaries of the North American continent, even the black frontier the Confederates had tried to establish in '61? Now all that was left was the open south, the only door open to his encounter with the fifth, blind, murderous blow of fate.

Dawn rose over the edge of the mountain.

"Is this the way to Chihuahua?" he asked his fat host.

The Mexican nodded and in turn asked with a jealous glance toward the closed door of his house: "And what takes you to Chihuahua, mister?"

Speaking in Spanish, he added a faint *ee* that made the word sound like *misteree*, and the old man thought how the first advantage a gringo always has over a Mexican is that of being a mystery, something he doesn't know how to take: friend or enemy. Although generally they didn't get the benefit of the doubt.

The Mexican continued: "The fighting is thick around there; that's Pancho Villa territory."

His look was more eloquent than his words. The old man thanked him and set off. Behind him, he heard the Mexican open the door to scold the woman, who only then had dared to peer outside. The gringo thought he could imagine the black melancholy of her eyes; a journey is painful for the one who has to remain behind, but more beautiful than it can ever be for the traveler. The old gringo tried to reject the comforting notion that his presence in another man's house might still provoke jealousy.

The mountains rose like worn, dark-skinned fists and the old man imagined the body of Mexico as a gigantic corpse with bones of silver, eyes of gold, flesh of stone, and balls hard as copper.

The mountains were the fists. He was going to pry them open, one after the other, hoping that sooner or later, like an ant scurrying along the furrowed palm, he would find what he was after.

That night he tied his horse to an enormous organ-pipe cactus and fell into a famished sleep, thankful for his woolen underwear. He dreamed about what he had seen before falling asleep: new bluish stars and dying yellow ones. He tried to forget his dead children, wondering which of the stars were already quenched, their light nothing more than his own illusion: a heritage from the dead stars to human eyes that would continue to praise them centuries after their extinction in an ancient catastrophe of dust and flames.

He dreamed he was crossing a flaming bridge. He awakened. He wasn't dreaming. He'd seen the bridge that morning as he crossed into Mexico. But now as he gazed at the stars the old man said to himself: "My eyes shine brighter than any star. No one will ever see me old and decrepit. I will always be young because today I dare to be young again. I will always be remembered as I was."

Steel-blue eyes beneath speckled, almost blond, eyebrows. They were not the best defense against the raging sun and the raw wind that the following day bore him into the heart of the desert, occasionally nibbling on a dry sandwich, settling a shapeless wide-brimmed black Stetson lower on his thatch of silvery hair. He felt like a gigantic albino monster in a world the sun had reserved for its favored, a people of shadow protected by darkness. The wind died down but the sun continued to burn. By afternoon, his skin would be peeling. He was deep in the Mexican desert, sister to the Sahara and the Gobi, continuation of the Arizona and Yuma deserts, mirror of the belt of sterile splendors girdling the globe as if to remind it that cold sands, burning skies, and barren beauty wait patiently and alertly to again overcome the earth from its very womb: the desert.

"The old gringo came to Mexico to die."

And nevertheless, plodding steadily forward on the white mare, he felt that his wish to die was a mockery. He surveyed the desert around him. Agave rose wiry and sharp as a sword's point. On every branch of the candlewood tree, thorns protected the untouchable beauty of a savagely red flower. The desert willow concentrated in a single pale, purplish flower all the sweetness of its nauseating perfume. The choya grew capricious and tall, shielding its yellow blossoms. The gringo may have come in search of Villa and the Revolution, but the desert was already the image of war: Spanish bayonet, war-like Apache plumes, and the aggressive, hook-like thorns of the palo verde. The desert's advance guard were its ranks of tumbleweed, botanical brothers to the packs of nocturnal wolves.

Buzzards circled above; the old man raised his head, then alertly looked toward the ground. In the desert, scorpions and snakes strike only at strangers. A traveler is always a stranger. Dazed, he looked up, then down; he heard the mournful song of dark doves, swift as arrows, was confused by the flight of peregrine falcons. High overhead, birds trailed a sound like dry, rustling grass.

He closed his eyes but did not spur his horse.

Then the desert told him that death is nothing more than the exhaustion of the laws of nature: life is the rule of the game, not its exception, and even the seemingly dead desert hid a minute world of life that originated, prolonged, imitated the laws of human existence. He could not free himself—even if he wanted to—from the vital imperative of the barrenness to which he had come of his own free will, without anyone's having commanded: Old gringo, get you to the desert.

Sand mounts the mesquite. The horizon shimmers and rises before the eyes. Implacable shadows of clouds clothe the earth in dotted veils. Earth smells fill the air. A rainbow spills into a mirror of itself. Thickets of snakeweed blaze in clustered yellow blooms. Everything is blasted by an alkaline wind.

The old gringo coughs, covers his face with a black scarf. His breathing ebbs, as long ago the waters had drawn back from the earth to create the desert. He thirsts for air as salt cedars on parched stream banks treasure moisture.

He has to stop, choked by asthma, dismount painfully, gasping for breath, and devoutly sink his face into the mare's flank. In spite of everything, he says: "I am in control of my destiny."

4

Inocencio Mansalvo said as soon as he saw the gringo approaching the encampment: "That man came here to die."

As Pedro was only eleven and still a long way from being on equal terms with a brave guerrilla like the man from Torreón, Coahuila, he didn't understand very well what Inocencio meant. But from that moment the gringo had all his respect. Mansalvo may have been a lion in battle, but he was even more deadly when it came to predicting a person's fate. And as it turned out, the old gringo was braver than anyone in the battles fought in Chihuahua. Maybe Mansalvo sensed the gringo's suicidal courage the minute he saw him and that's why he said what he said.

"That gringo comes riding in here as if he was ready for a fight, as if he wanted to take us all on, even if it meant we jump him and cut him in little pieces."

"You can see that he is a man of honor; he comes with no bad intentions," said Colonel Frutos García, whose father was a Spaniard. "You can see that at once."

"I tell you, he's come to die," Inocencio insisted.

"But with honor," repeated the Colonel.

"I don't know about 'with honor,' since he's a gringo. But die, yes," Mansalvo said once again. "What does a gringo expect from us but that, death?"

"Why does it have to be so?"

Inocencio's teeth shone so brightly that his eyes glowed green. "Because he crossed the frontier. Isn't that reason enough?"

"My God, no," said La Garduña, laughing—an appalling whore from Durango who'd attached herself to the troops, the only professional among the many decent women following the forces of "our" General Arroyo. "What he's doing is praying. He must be a holy man." She laughed so hard the paint on her fat cheeks cracked like varnish dried in the sun. She buried her nose in a bunch of dead roses she always wore pinned to her breast.

Later, in the few days he rode with the Villa troops, both Inocencio and the Colonel found that the old gringo was as careful about his looks as a young girl getting ready for her first dance. He had his own razor and kept it carefully honed; he rummaged through the camp until he found boiling water to get the smoothest shave; he even—the old peacock!—got to where he expected a warm towel. But oh, if he was clumsy and cut himself!—though he had a good mirror at his disposal in General Arroyo's railroad car. None of the rest of us ever shaved looking in a mirror, always by feel, or at the most in the flowing mirror of a river. But oh, if that old man nicked himself, what a caper he cut: he turned even paler; he dabbed at it as if he were going to bleed to death; he pulled out some tiny white papers and quickly covered the wound, as if he cared less about the bleeding or infection than he did about his looks.

"The thing is, he's never been dead before in all his

life," screeched La Garduña, looking less as if she'd come from a whorehouse in Durango than from the holy ground next to it where priests refused to bury women like her.

"All of you say that Death sent him," she said, sneezing, as if her flowers were still fresh. "I say the devil sent him, because not even the devil wants him. What's he doing here? He's got to be as poor as all of you or as fucked up as me or as mean . . . as himself."

"He looks like he's praying, looking for something," Mansalvo said from a distance.

"He has a sorrow in his eyes," La Garduña said suddenly, and from that moment respected him.

He was finally there, in sight of the plain, after four days of solitary slogging across the dry land: a plain dotted with smoking camps scattered like creosote brush around a paralyzed train squatting on the rails. As he trotted now through the sagebrush, the scene lay before him: railroad cars like rolling homes for the women and children of the soldiers resting on the roofs of the coaches and smoking loosely rolled, yellowish cigarettes.

He'd made it.

He was finally here. Cantering, he asked himself whether he really knew anything about this country. Like lightning, through his blue eyes flashed the distant image of the editorial room of the *San Francisco Chronicle*, where news of Mexico hovered lazily through the air, unlike the arrows that kept the reporters hopping: local scandals, national events; the reporters of William Randolph Hearst's empire were energetic American Achilleses, not Mexican tortoises, swift on the trail of news, inventing news if necessary. News stories, trophies of the hunt, burst through the windows of the Hearst editorial room: in Wisconsin, La Follette elected on a populist platform; Upton Sinclair publishes *The Jungle*; Taft inaugurated, promising tariff reforms; and an ancient, bemedaled pharaoh was ensconced in Chapultepec Castle, saying evening after evening, "Kill them, while they're hot!" and keeping himself alive only by maintaining a vigilant and hostile eye on the buzzards circling the palaces and churches of Mexico. A vigilant old man, the delight of newspapermen, an aged tyrant with a genius for publishable phrases: "Poor Mexico, so far from God and so close to the United States." Trivial, irritating news items, news like fat green flies on a summer afternoon, buzzing into the newsroom of the *San Francisco Chronicle*, where sluggish big brown fans struggled vainly to stir the sultry air. Princeton University had produced Wilson; Teddy Roosevelt had split away to form the Bull Moose Party; and in Mexico, bandits named Carranza, Obregón, Villa, and Zapata had taken up arms with the secondary aim of avenging the death of Madero and overthrowing that drunken tyrant Victoriano Huerta, but with the principal aim of stealing Hearst's land. Wilson spoke of the New Freedom and said he would teach the Mexicans democracy. Hearst demanded: Intervention, War, Indemnification.

"You didn't have to come to Mexico to be killed, son," the shade of his father said to him. "Do you remember when you began writing? There were some who took bets on your longevity."

"What he's doing is, he's praying," said La Garduña. "He must be a holy man."

"They'll never bury you in holy ground," said Inocencio, laughing.

"Oh, no?" said La Garduña. "I have it all arranged with my family in Durango. When I die, they're going to say that I'm my Aunt Josefa Arreola. She was a virgin all her life, so pure no one remembers anything about her. Priests only remember sinners."

"Well, we'll see what side the gringo's on, the saints' or the sinners'."

"What can a gringo want from us?"

The old gringo knew there were swarms of newspapermen like him, from both coasts, prowling around Pancho Villa's army, so nobody stopped him as he rode through the camp. But they looked at him doubtfully: he didn't look like a newspaperman, Colonel Frutos García always said; and no wonder they would look so strangely at a tall, skinny old man, white-haired and blue-eyed, pink skin scored with wrinkles like the furrows of a corn field, legs hanging below his stirrups. As his father was a Spaniard and a businessman in Salamanca, Guanajuato, Frutos García said that that's how the goatherds and rough serving girls had looked at Don Quixote when he came poking into their villages without being invited, riding a bony old nag and with his lance charging armies of sorcerers.

"Doctor! Doctor!" they cried to him from the crowded boxcars as they spied the black bag.

"No. Not doctor. Villa. I am looking for Pancho Villa," the old man shouted back.

"Villa! Villa! Viva Villa!" they shouted in chorus, until a soldier in a sweat- and dirt-streaked yellow sombrero yelled, laughing, from the roof of a baggage car: "We are all Villa!"

The old gringo felt someone tugging at his trouser leg

and glanced down. A boy of eleven with eyes like black marbles and with two bandoliers slung across his chest said: "You want to meet Pancho Villa? The General is going to see him tonight. Come see the General, señor."

The boy took the reins of the old man's horse and led him toward one of the railroad cars, where a man with a strong jawbone, a sparse mustache, and narrow yellow eyes was eating tacos, blowing a lank, rebellious lock of copper hair from his eyes.

"Who're you, gringo? Another newspaperman?" asked the man with the slit eyes, swinging leather-legging-covered legs from the open door of the shunted car. "Or have you come to sell us supplies?"

"This man has come here looking for death," Inocencio Mansalvo wanted to tell his chief, but La Garduña clapped her hand over his mouth in time: she wanted to see if what her three friends thought that morning was true. The eleven-year-old led the stranger's horse.

The old man shook his head and said he'd come to join Villa's army. "I want to fight."

The slit eyes opened a fraction; the dusty mask split open in mirth. La Garduña echoed the laughter, and she was chorused by the women dressed in long ragged skirts who came from the kitchen at the far end of the baggage car, wrapped in their rebozos, to see what was making the General laugh so loud.

"Old man! Old man!" said the young general, laughing. "You're too old! Go water your garden, old man! What're you doing here? We don't need any dead weight. We shoot our prisoners of war to keep from having to haul them along with us. This is an army of guerrilla fighters, you understand what that is?"

"I came to fight," said the gringo.

"He came to die," said Inocencio Mansalvo.

"We move fast and make no noise; your hair would glow at night like a white flare, old man. Go away, leave us alone. This is an army, not a home for old men."

"Try me," said the old man, and he said it coldly, the Colonel remembers.

The women had been chirping like birds, but they fell silent when the General looked at the old man as coldly as the old man had spoken. The General pulled out a long Colt .44. The old man didn't stir in his saddle. Then the General threw him the pistol and the old man caught it on the fly.

They waited again. The General thrust his hand into the deep pocket of his white peasant's trousers, pulled out a shiny silver peso, big as an egg and flat as a watch, and tossed it straight and high in the air. The old man waited without moving until the coin fell to within a foot of the General's nose; then he fired; the women screamed; La Garduña looked at the other women; the Colonel and Inocencio looked at their chief; only the boy looked at the gringo.

The General barely flicked his head. The boy ran to look for the coin; he picked it out of the dust, rubbed the barely bent surface against his bandolier, and returned it to the General. A perfect hole pierced the body of the eagle.

"Keep the coin, Pedrito, you brought him to us," the General said, smiling, and the silver piece almost burned his fingers. "I don't think anything but a Colt .44 could have pierced a peso like that. It was my first treasure. You won it, Pedrito, you keep it."

"This man came to die," said Mansalvo.

"Now I'm not so sure he is a holy man," said La Garduña, sniffing her roses.

What is a gringo doing in Mexico, the Colonel asked himself.

"His eyes were filled with prayers"—now she sits alone and remembers—and if the old gringo did not read the minds of those who watched as he descended from the metallic mountains to the desert, he repeated his own written words to them from afar: "This fragment of humanity, this type and example of acute sensation, this handiwork of man and beast, this humble, unheroic Prometheus, comes praying, yes, imploring everything for the boon of oblivion.

"To the earth and sky alike, to the vegetation of the desert, to whatever took form in sense or consciousness, this incarnate suffering addressed that silent plea: 'I have come to die. Give me the coup de grâce.'"

 The old gringo smiled as General Tomás Arroyo puffed at the lock of copper hair falling over his eyes and thrust out his lower lip to draw a breath of air before jumping to the ground and planting himself, fists on hips, before the stranger: "I am General Tomás Arroyo."

He shot out the name firmly, but the personal dart was the military title, and from that instant the gringo knew that all the commonplaces of Mexican machismo would be rained upon his white head, one after another, until they found how far they could go with him; testing him, yes, but also masking themselves before him, refusing to show him their true faces.

They cheered him after his feat with the Colt .44 and gave him a new broad-brimmed sombrero; they forced tacos on him, with burning-hot chilis and blood sausage; they showed him the bottle of mescal with the fat worm settled at the bottom of the liquor, meant to test the stomach of the queasy.

"So we have a gringo general with us."

"Topographical engineer," said the old man. "Ninth Regiment of the Indiana Volunteers. North American Civil War."

"Civil War! But that was over fifty years ago, when we were busy defending ourselves against the French."

"What's in these tacos?"

"Bull's testicles and blood, Indiana General. You'll need both if you join the army of Pancho Villa."

"And what's in the alcohol?"

"Don't worry, Indiana General. The little worm is not alive. It just lengthens the life of the mescal."

The women served the tacos. Arroyo and his boys exchanged glances, their faces perfectly blank. The old gringo ate in silence, swallowing the chilis whole; his eyes didn't water and his face didn't turn red. Gringos complain that they get sick in Mexico. But no Mexican dies of diarrhea from eating or drinking in his own country. It's like this bottle, said Arroyo. If the bottle and you carry the little worm all your life, the two of you grow old like good comrades. The worm eats some things and you eat others. But if you eat things like I saw in El Paso, food wrapped in paper and sealed so not even a fly can touch it, then the worm will attack you because you don't know him and he doesn't know you, Indiana General.

The old gringo decided he could wait with all the patience in the world—all the patience of his dispassionate Protestant ancestors assured of salvation through faith—for General Tomás Arroyo to offer him the face the world didn't know.

They were in the General's private car, which reminded the old gringo of the interior of one of the whorehouses he'd liked to visit in New Orleans. He sank into a deep red velvet armchair and sardonically stroked the tassels of the gold-lamé curtains. The chandelier hanging precariously above their heads tinkled as the train began chugging down the track. Young General Arroyo tossed down his glass of mescal, and the old man, without a word, imitated him.

The old gringo's mocking gaze as he surveyed the sumptuous carriage with its lacquered walls and tufted ceiling had not escaped Arroyo's notice. The old gringo was keeping a tight rein on his natural banter and irony, constantly reminding himself: "Not yet."

What is strange is that from the beginning he also felt the need to control a different sentiment—a paternal affection for Arroyo. He wanted to curb both, but Arroyo, his own eyes invisible behind narrow slits, saw only (or wanted to see only) the look of contained mockery. The train seemed determined that this was not the moment to be halted; it worked up to a steady pace, making its way through the desolate dusk of the desert, moving away from mountains that still testified to the titanic struggle in which some had engendered others, tilted against each other to hold themselves upright, grumbling at times, lifting enormous red- and gold-

[26]

crowned towers into the dusk, their hulking bodies striated in blues and greens. Now the silent sea of the desert lay at their feet and from the car window the old man could recognize and name the furtive growth of the smoke tree.

Arroyo told him that the train had belonged to a very wealthy family, owners of half the state of Chihuahua and parts of Durango and Coahuila as well. Had the gringo really looked at the troops who greeted his arrival? For example, an innocent-looking guy with dirt on his Stetson, and a disreputable whore? He must have noticed the boy who led him here, the one he had told he could keep the blistering peso with the decapitated eagle? Well, now this train belonged to them. Arroyo said he could understand why such a train was needed—he said it with a kind of bilious grimace—since it took two days and a night to cross the Miranda family estate.

"The owners?" the old man asked, his face wooden.

"Prove it!" Arroyo barked.

The old man shrugged his shoulders. "You just said it. This is their estate."

"But not their property."

It was one thing to take something, something that isn't yours, the way the Miranda family had taken this cattle country in the north surrounded by a desert they wanted sterile and harsh for their own protection, a wall of sun and mesquite enclosing the land they had grabbed, said Arroyo. But it was something else to be the true owner because you had worked for it. His hand fell from the gold curtain and he asked the old man to count his calluses. The gringo said he could sympathize that the General had been a peon on the Miranda hacienda and now he was getting even, riding around in the flashy private railroad car that had once belonged to his masters. Wasn't that how it was?

"You don't understand, gringo," said Arroyo in a thick and incredulous voice. "You really don't understand. Our papers are older than theirs."

He walked to a strongbox hidden behind a row of soft damask cushions, opened it, and removed a long flat box of worn green velveteen and splintered rosewood. He opened it before the old man's eyes.

The General and the gringo looked at the papers as brittle as old silk.

The General and the gringo looked at each other in silence, communicating from opposite sides of a deep chasm: the looks were their words, and the land flowing past the train window behind each of them told the story of the papers, which was the story of Arroyo, and also the history in the books, which was the story of the gringo. (The old man thought with a bitter smile: papers for both, in the end, but the manner of knowing them, not knowing them, preserving them, was so different: *This archive of the desert is flowing along and I don't know where it will stop, I don't know*, that much the old gringo accepted, *but I know what I want*.) He saw in Arroyo's eyes what Arroyo was telling him in different words, he saw in the passing Chihuahua landscape, in its tragic gesture of loss, less than Arroyo could tell him but more than he himself knew. This was one gringo who would not set foot in a land before he knew the history of that land; this gringo would know the last detail of the land he had chosen to receive his seventy-one years of bone and hide. As if the story kept flowing without interrupting the rhythm of the train, or the

[28]

rhythm of Arroyo's memory (the gringo knew that Arroyo was remembering, but he only knew: the Mexican stroked the papers as he would stroke his mother's cheek, or the curve of his lover's hip), each watched the advances, the retreats, the movements in the eyes of the other: flee from the Spanish, flee from the Indians, flee from the servile labor of the *encomienda*, accept the great cattle ranches as the lesser evil, preserve like precious islands the few communal lands, the rights to land and water guaranteed in Nueva Vizcaya by the Spanish Crown, avoid forced labor and, for a few, seek to preserve the communal property granted by the King, resist being rustlers or slaves or rebels or displaced Indians, but finally, even they, the strongest, the most honorable, the most humble and at the same time the most proud, conquered by a destiny of defeat: slaves and rustlers, never free men, except by being rebels. That was the story of this land and the old bookworm of American libraries knew it and looked into Arroyo's eyes to confirm that the General knew it, too: slaves or rustlers, never free men, and yet possessors of the right that allowed them to be free: their rebellion.

"You see, gringo General? You see what's written here? You see the writing? You see the precious red seal? These lands have always been ours, *ours*, a handful of hardworking men granted protection against the *encomienda* system and against the attacks of the Toboso Indians. The King of Spain himself said so. Even he acknowledged it was ours. It says so right here. Written in his own hand. This is his signature. I am the keeper of these papers. The papers prove that no one else has a right to these lands."

"My dear General, you can read?" the gringo asked, a glinting smile in his gaze. The mescal was fiery stuff that stirred his worst instincts. But it also stirred his paternal feelings. Arroyo grasped the gringo's hand forcefully, though not threateningly. He almost patted it, and it was a surge of affection that snapped the old man brutally from his halfhearted parry, bringing thoughts, and sudden, dizzying pain, of his own two sons. The General said, Look outside before the sun sets, look at the land they were leaving behind, the twisted, thirsty sculptures of plants struggling to conserve water, as if to tell the rest of the dying desert that there was hope, and that in spite of all appearances they were not yet dead.

"You think that organ-pipe cactus can read and I can't? You are a fool, gringo. I may not be able to read, but I can remember. I cannot read the papers I have in safekeeping for my people; our Colonel Frutos García does me the favor of reading them for me. But I know what my papers mean better than any who can read. You understand?"

The old man replied only that it is the law of the marketplace that property should change hands; no wealth can develop from stagnant property. On the side toward the window, he felt a glow on his cheek, and for a minute believed that the warmth was his own reaction to the terror sparked by the sun each evening as it abandons us: its terror and ours. He stared straight into the fierce yellow eyes of Tomás Arroyo. Repeatedly, the General tapped his brow with his forefinger: all the stories, all the histories, are here in my head, a whole library of words; the history of my people, my village, our pain: here in my head.

"I know who I am, old man. Do you?"

It wasn't the vanished sunlight that burned the gringo's cheek through the window. It was a fire on the plain. The vanished sun had been replaced by fire.

"Ah, those boys of mine." General Arroyo sighed with a kind of pride. He ran toward the rear platform. The old man followed with as much dignity as he could muster.

"Ah, those boys. They got here ahead of me." He pointed toward the fire and said, Look, old man, the glory of the Mirandas going up in smoke. He had told his boys he would be there by dusk. They had got there ahead of him. But they were not robbing him of his pleasure; they knew this was his pleasure, that he should arrive as the hacienda was going up in flames.

"Good planning, gringo."

"A bad business, General."

As the train pulled into the station of the Miranda hacienda, a band was playing the *Zacatecas March*. The gringo could not distinguish the smell of the burning hacienda from the smell of burnt tortillas. A thick, ashy haze enveloped men and women, children and improvised kitchens, horses and stray cattle, trains and abandoned wagons. Colonel García's and Inocencio Mansalvo's shouted orders could be heard above the indistinguishable sounds of the other, almost natural, uproar.

"Guard, halt . . . !"

"Maize for our general's horse!"

"Brigade, at-ten-*shun!*"

"We'll really live it up tonight!"

Dogs were barking as General Arroyo descended from

the railroad carriage, his enormous sombrero heavy with embroidered silver vine leaves set like a war crown above his shadowed face. He looked up and for the first time saw fear on the old gringo's face. The dogs' barking was for the stranger, who hesitated to take the next step and jump to the ground.

"Here, Mansalvo," he ordered, "get those dogs away from the gringo general." Then he smiled, "Oh, my brave gringo. The Federal soldiers are far more savage than these sickly mongrels."

There was no pleasure in Arroyo's face as the old gringo followed, his tall, ungainly body contrasting with the shorter, younger, more dramatically muscular form of the General, who was walking across the dusty flat beyond the station toward the flaming compound of main house and buildings amid a metallic clatter of spurs and belts and pistols and rapidly retired artillery and the rising murmur of the desert breeze playing over the only leaves in sight—the silver leaves on the General's sombrero.

A whistling sound settled over everything as the old gringo stared with atavistic horror at the row of hanged men strung on the telegraph poles, mouths agape, tongues protruding. They were all whistling, swinging in the soft desert breeze, all along the avenue leading to the burning hacienda.

6 She was there. In the middle of the crowd, struggling and pushing and trying to find her place, gazing at the faces that blurred into one, wanting to be a witness to the spectacle. From the middle of the silent throng of sombreros and rebozos emerged those gray eyes fighting to retain a sense of their own identity, of personal dignity and courage in the midst of the vertiginous terror of the unexpected.

The old man saw her for the first time, and said to himself: She must have been forewarned.

And yet there she was, no doubt stubborn as a mule and not very realistic; seeing her, he recognized in her many comparable girls he had known in his lifetime, including his wife when she was young, and his beautiful daughter. He asked himself what he might have associated her with had he met her somewhere else, and "somewhere else" meant: the proper place, circumstances natural to her. To a proper young lady. No, more than that, a young lady with proper manners trying to follow her mother's instructions and become a cultivated woman. A young matron, before long. Not yet, but no longer dependent on pin money.

What would she say? What could he expect of her? What were her commonplaces, like the General's blood sausage and fat little worm? "I am an American citizen. I demand to see my consul. I have certain constitutional rights. You cannot detain me here. You do not know with whom you are dealing." No. None of those things. They were forcibly detaining her because the hacienda was on fire, and maybe in their bones they felt something telling them she had come here to work and live and stay and no one was going to fumigate her like a common insect and run her off the place where she had been employed, for which she had already been paid a month's wages in advance.

This, in effect, is what she was saying, in an accent the old man placed in the East, on the Atlantic coast, doubtlessly New York, but immediately drifted south-ward—the lightest intonation of Virginia superimposed on Manhattan. At any rate, only he seemed to under-stand what she was saying, and maybe the General, a little; he had been in El Paso, he said, maybe in exile, maybe running guns.

"I have received my salary and I shall stay here until the family returns and I am able to instruct the children in the English tongue and earn my salary. So there!"

Arroyo looked at her with a grin specifically intended to instill fear, but immediately dissolved into laughter; a foolish laugh, but powerful, young, and imbued with profound experience of human stupidity; the old man would always say that at that moment Arroyo reminded him of a tragic clown—a buffoon who had to be taken seriously. Arroyo interpreted the woman's words for his people. The men laughed openly; the women made muffled bird sounds behind their rebozos. She says she is going to teach English to the little Mirandas, did you hear that? She thinks they will return, did you hear? Come on, Inocencio, tell her the truth; they will never return, señorita, they left just in time for Paris, France, the minute they felt the flames licking closer they sold the hacienda and bought a big house over there; they will never return, shrieked La Garduña, complacently waggling her breasts with the bunch of dry flowers, they were just having fun with you, señorita, they got you here for nothing; just to make us believe they were not leaving, Colonel Frutos García said in a more restrained tone—and La Garduña: "They left us all whistling on the hill, se-ño-rrrrita!"

"Which means, up the creek," the old man said in English. She looked at him. It was difficult to see anyone in the confusion of smoke and fire and foreign faces, but she looked toward him.

"Help me," she murmured.

The old man knew it was not easy for her to say this, to ask for anyone's help; he saw it in her chin, in her eyes, in the rising and falling of her breast. He knew then and there it was up to him to see through this girl's actions and words, respecting both; but she was not trying to deceive anyone, she was only attempting to come to terms with herself, with the struggle that he could see in all her feminine transparency. He looked at her and thought: I know all about her, but she has every right to hide who she is from me and I have the obligation to respect it. An independent girl, not rich, not comfortable; and not for want of pin money, or family education. Uncomfortable, because she is here the same as I, fighting for her very being. She was transparent, and the gringo, as he looked at her, told himself that maybe he was transparent, too, after all. There are people whose external reality is generous because it is transparent, because you can read everything, accept everything, understand everything about them: people who carry their own sun with them.

Arroyo looked at them from behind slit eyelids, the gringo first, then the gringo woman. Arroyo was opaque; his opacity was his virtue, the old man thought as he observed him. His generosity was his enigma: for him to be understood or to give of himself, you had to probe deep below the surface. Half of the world is transparent; the other half, opaque. Arroyo: something swift and hidden behind that raccoon mask; something racing deep within his brain.

"Well. You take care of her, Indiana General. You see that she keeps out of harm."

Arroyo was borne away on the groundswell of his people and they remained alone, two people staring intently at each other—the old man vigilant, wary of his journalist's tendency to form the instant stereotype that enabled the stupid masses to understand in a flash and feel flattered for it; a tag for everything, that was the Bible of his boss, Mr. Hearst. He walked a few inches behind the woman, ostensibly to make her feel protected but in reality observing her, her manner of walking, her manner of carrying herself, the small, revealing gestures of wounded pride, followed by resolute spasms of self-assertion. For his newspaper he would have written, electing one of the extremes that so delighted Hearst, a loose woman masquerading as a schoolmistress, or a schoolmistress in search of the first real adventure of her life. Although he could also adopt the perspective of a gentleman from the cotton states and ask himself simply whether this Northern girl knew what chivalry was.

She stopped, hesitant, before a closed glass door. The old man stepped forward just as she reached out to take the doorknob and open the door herself.

"Allow me, ma'am," said the old man, and she accepted. She was pleased; she, too, had her prejudices. And she was no longer, as they say, in the springtime of her life.

They found themselves standing in a ballroom. The old man did not look around the hall. He looked at her, and mentally chastised himself for this fever of perception. She, more composed, looked around and suggested a corner where they could sit down and exchange information and names—she was Harriet Winslow, from Washington, D.C. He did not give his name; he said merely: I am from San Francisco, California—and she repeated her story: she had come to teach the English language to the three children of the Miranda family.

Now, as he looked at her, he saw her really for the first time, not transparent and essential, but circumstantially opaque. Harriet Winslow arranged her tie and smoothed the wrinkles of her pleated skirt as if she were a woman somehow separate from herself, a woman dressed in the uniform of American working girls: a typical Gibson Girl. No, she was not exactly in the springtime of her life, but she was still young, beautiful, and, now she knew, independent, not destined to pass from her mother's cradle to that of her husband. Her life was not rose-colored, not pampered, not for the moment. Maybe sometime, if those unique traits had not been acquired but learned at her mother's breast. The quick, sure elegance of a beautiful woman of thirty.

They did not speak about themselves. She did not tell him the circumstances that brought her to Mexico. He did not tell her that he had come here to die because everything he loved had died before him. They did not even say what was on each of their tongues. They did not utter the word "escape" because they did not want to admit they were prisoners.

The old man said only: "Nothing is holding you here,

[37]

you know. You are not responsible for a revolution or for the flight of your employers. The money belongs to you."

"But I did not earn it, sir."

Their words sounded hollow. No one had to tell them that they were prisoners for them to feel trapped by the foreignness of the place, the smells, the sounds, the drunken celebration that sounded closer now; the closed fist of the desert.

"I am sure the General will assist you in finding transport, ma'am."

"What general?"

"You know. The one who asked me to look after you."

"General?" Harriet's large eyes opened wide. "He doesn't look like any general I have ever known."

"You mean, he doesn't look like a gentleman."

"As you wish; but he does not resemble a general, gentleman or not. Who appointed him general? I am sure he named himself."

"That happens sometimes, in extraordinary circumstances. But you seem truly offended, ma'am."

She looked at him, half smiling. "I'm sorry. I do not wish to sound prejudiced. It's just that I'm nervous. You see, the army means a great deal to me."

"Well, I don't want to seem inquisitive either, but it is difficult for me, at first sight, to connect you with . . ."

"Oh, not I myself, you understand. My father. He disappeared during the Spanish-American War. The army lent him dignity, and us as well. Without the army, he would have been dependent on charity. And we. My mother and I, I mean."

Then this instructress for a hacienda that no longer existed, this schoolmistress of children she had never met and knew nothing about, not even if they existed, shook her head like a wounded bird, and the celebration of the troops burst upon the ballroom where the two Americans had taken refuge. There were coyote-like whoops and the quiet laughter of Indians, who never laugh loudly, like the Spaniards, or with resentment, like the mestizos.

Secret laughter and an out-of-tune trumpet. Then sudden silence.

"They have seen us," Harriet murmured, drawing close to the old man's side.

They had seen themselves.

The Miranda ballroom was a miniature Versailles. The walls were two long rows of mirrors, ceiling to floor: a gallery of mirrors destined to reproduce in a round of perpetual pleasures the elegant steps and movements of couples from Chihuahua, El Paso, and other haciendas, come to dance the waltz and the quadrille on the elegant parquet Señor Miranda had had brought from France.

The men and women of Arroyo's troops were looking at themselves. Paralyzed by their own images, by the full-length reflection of their being, by the wholeness of their bodies. They turned slowly, as if to make sure this was not just another illusion. They were caught in the labyrinth of mirrors. The old man realized that he and Miss Harriet had not even noticed the mirrors when they entered, both doubtlessly conditioned to ballrooms, he to the large modern hotels built in San Francisco following the great earthquake; she to some military ball in Washington at the elegant invitation of her beau.

The old man shook his head; no, he had not seen the mirrors when he entered, because he had eyes only for Miss Harriet.

One of Arroyo's soldiers held an arm toward the mirror. "Look, it's you."

And his companion pointed toward the reflection in the other mirror. "It's me."

"It's us."

The words made the rounds—it's us, it's us—followed by the sound of a guitar joined by many voices, and the cavalry troops came in, and once again there was entertainment and dancing and gaiety—indifferent to the presence of the two gringos—in the hacienda of the Mirandas. Then an accordion struck up a *norteña* polka, and as they danced, the spurs of the horsemen scratched and splintered the fine parquet floor. The old man restrained Harriet's impulsive gesture.

"It's their party," the old man said. "Don't get into it."

Angrily, she wrested her hands from his. "They are ruining the parquet."

He held her arm, irritated. "You didn't pay for it. I tell you, don't get involved."

"I am responsible!" exclaimed Harriet Winslow, stiff with pride. "Señor Miranda paid me a month in advance. I shall be responsible for seeing that his property is respected during his absence. I tell you, I am responsible."

"So you don't plan to return home, ma'am?"

She smiled as he might have, had he not already defined his reasons for never again returning home.

"Of course not! After all I have seen here tonight!"

She took a deep, deep breath. She told him she had graduated from normal school with high marks, but then she realized that she did not like giving lessons to children who already thought the things she taught them. She lacked challenge, stimulation. To have remained in

[40]

the United States would have been to succumb to routine. She felt it was her duty to come to Mexico.

"Since the children I came to instruct have left, I shall stay here and instruct these children," she said in a tone of voice in which shame and pride were revealed in equal measure.

The men and women of the troops and from the village mingled together, danced, and exchanged furtive kisses, remote now from the disturbing sense of that other presence: themselves in the mirrors.

"You don't know them. You don't know them at all," said the old man, trying to contain a feeling for her he did not want to feel: compassionate scorn, a reminder of his former self, before his decision to come to Mexico.

He spread another thought on this one, like butter on toast: When they entered the ballroom, had Harriet Winslow looked at herself in the mirrors? But she was replying to his assertion, her confidence completely recovered: *And they do not know me!*

"Look at them, what these people need is education, not rifles. A good scrubbing, followed by a few lessons on how we do things in the United States, and you'd see an end to this chaos."

"You're going to civilize them?" the old man asked dryly.

"Precisely. And starting tomorrow."

"Wait a little," the old man said. "They say *mañana* in Spanish, and whatever you do, you have to sleep somewhere tonight."

"I have already told you, I intend to take charge of this place until the legitimate owners return. Wouldn't you do the same?"

"There is no 'place.' It's burned to the ground. The

owners aren't coming back. You aren't going to stay to educate anyone. They would likely educate you first, Miss Winslow, and not in a very pleasant way."

She looked at him in surprise. "I thought you were a gentleman, sir."

"I am, ma'am, I swear to you, I am, and that is why I'm going to look after you."

He swept her up like a doll, lifted her from the ruined parquet to his old but still strong shoulders, and carried her outside, choking with surprise, multiplied as if in a shimmering silver dream in a forest of mirrors; he carried her from the bubble of music and glass so mysteriously respected, saved from the fire set by the General's orders, two gringos retreating amid jeering and howls of celebration: the hoopla of victory: she, struggling and kicking in the cold desert air as he made his way among the bonfires and the smoke of dung and tortillas.

"You take care of her, Indiana General."

He suddenly realized that the only refuge he had was the protection offered by the dark and arrogant General Arroyo. The gringo had fallen into the young revolutionary's trap. He had been about to carry Harriet Winslow to that ostentatious railway carriage, to the private bordello of an illiterate guerrilla whose head might have been filled with memories of injustice but who was nevertheless a man who did not even know how to read and write. He looked at Harriet Winslow, asking her what he was asking himself. Was the woman right?

Carefully, he set her down and held her briefly before looking around him at the men and women of the revolutionary army of Chihuahua, wrapped in their serapes around the campfires.

Harriet and the gringo stared at each other, disconsolate, each reflecting the desolation in the eyes of the other. The desert at night is a great open-air dome, the largest bedchamber in the world. Arms about each other, they felt as if they were sinking to the bottom of a great bed: the bed of the ocean that once had occupied this platter of coarse sand and then drawn back, leaving a wasteland inhabited by all the specters of water: seas, oceans, all existing or possible rivers.

"Harriet, when we entered the ballroom, did you look at yourself in the mirror?"

"I don't know. Why?"

She wanted to ask him: Are you in this fighting, too? What is your place here? Before they burned down the hacienda, everyone had told her that this was a crucial campaign, that they had to move quickly, boldly, or the Revolution was lost. All the Federal soldiers they found, they hanged from the telegraph poles. They're whistling, do you hear them? It's terrible. Are you one of them? Are you fighting with them? Are you in danger of dying here?

The old man only repeated his question: "Did you look at yourself in the mirror?"

She didn't answer because just then a small woman wrapped in a blue rebozo, her face as round as the vanished moon, her eyes like sad almonds, came out of the General's car and said that the señorita was to sleep with her. The General was waiting for the old man. Tomorrow they would fight.

[43]

7

"What does she do now?"

"Now she sits alone and remembers."

"No. Now she sleeps."

"She dreams, in her dreams she is ageless."

"She thinks when she dreams that her dream will be her destiny."

"She dreams that an old man (her father?) is going to kiss her while she sleeps, before he goes away to war."

"He never returned from Cuba."

"There's an empty grave in Arlington."

"When I die, I want to be free of humiliation, resentment, guilt, or suspicion; mistress of myself, with my own opinions but without being sanctimonious or a pharisee."

"Your father went to Cuba and now you're going to Mexico. What a mania the Winslows have for back yards."

"Look at the map of our back yard: Here is Cuba. Here is Mexico. Here is Santo Domingo. Here is Honduras. Here is Nicaragua."

"I will never be able to understand our neighbors. We invite them to dinner and then they refuse to stay and wash the dishes."

"Look at the map, children. Learn."

"Loneliness is an absence of time."

"Wake up, Harriet, wake up. It's late."

Her mother always said that as a girl she'd been stubborn as a mule, but not very realistic, a bad combination for a young woman who had no dowry, especially if her behavior was not the coolest or most impeccable.

When she read the advertisement in the *Washington Star*, her heart began to pound. Why not? Teaching her primary-school classes had become routine, like attending church with her mother every Sunday, or the chaperoned outings over the last eight years with her just-turned-forty-two beau.

"After a certain age, society accepts you for what you are, as long as nothing changes and there are no surprises."

Why not! she asked herself, nibbling on the tie of her Gibson Girl outfit: white shirtwaist with leg-of-mutton sleeves and a high collar; tie; full, long wool skirt; high-button boots. Why *not*! After all, because of her, her mother was happy; she felt she had not been abandoned in her old age and appreciated the fact that her only daughter still slept under the same roof as her and accompanied her every Sunday to services in the Methodist church on Fifteenth Street, and Delaney, her beau, was happy because he had not been forced to give up his comfortable accommodations at his club, with all the customary services and minimal expenses of bachelor life, or jeopardize the necessary independence of a man who lobbied for special interests before the United States government.

"It's not safe anywhere in the world," Delaney would say as he read the daily headlines about the war clouds gathering over Europe.

"Why do you stay on here with me?" her mother would ask with a sweetly malicious smile. "You're thirty-one. Aren't you bored?"

Then she would kiss her daughter's cheek, forcing her to bow her head until she touched the mother's withered skin. And thus captive in the filial embrace, she had to listen to her mother's lament, yes, she could imagine the sorrow of a young girl who might have grown up wealthy in New York but instead had to go on waiting like her mother; waiting for news that never came, all her life. I wonder whether we've come into an inheritance? I wonder whether Papa died in Cuba? I wonder whether some young man will come to ask you out? No, it wasn't easy, because they wouldn't accept charity, isn't that right, daughter? and no young man would come to call on the penniless daughter of a widow of a captain in the United States Army, forced to leave New York and study in a Washington, D.C., normal school in order to be near—God knows why!—the source of army pensions, the memory of the father who'd been stationed there all those years, Arlington Cemetery where he should have been buried with full honors, except that no one knew where he was, where he fell during the Cuban campaign.

Beleaguered during a Washington summer, where if the vegetation was neglected for a moment the jungle would take over, swallowing up the entire city beneath a luxuriant growth of tropical plants, climbing vines, and rotting magnolias.

"The human response to the tropical jungle of Washington was to construct a pantheon worthy of Greece and Rome."

When she decided to leave, she took her mother's hand and her mother murmured: A cultivated young lady, but stubborn as a mule and unrealistic besides. In spite of everything, she said, sighing, I hope you will be happy; in spite of everything, she repeated, and in spite of our differences of opinion.

"You are not listening to me, Mama."

"Of course I am, daughter. I know everything. Here. This letter came for you."

The envelope was postmarked Mexico. It said clearly: *Miss Harriet Winslow, 2400 Fourteenth Street, Washington, D.C., United States of America.*

"Why did you open it, Mama? Who . . . ?"

She didn't want to finish the sentence, she didn't want
to argue. She decided to accept the offer from the
Miranda family before something happened, before her
mother died, or her father returned, or Delaney was tried
for federal fraud, she swears, she swears to herself. She
was determined to go to Mexico because she felt as if
she had already taught little American boys and girls
everything she could. She read that advertisement in the
Star and thought how in Mexico she would be able to
teach everything she knew to Mexican children. That
was the challenge she needed, she decided one day as
she donned her lacquered, black-ribboned straw hat. Her
knowledge of Spanish was a normal-school-trained teacher's minimal homage to a father fallen in Cuba. It would
serve her in teaching English to the children of the
Miranda family on a hacienda in Chihuahua.

"Don't go, Harriet. Don't forsake me now."

"I had made up my mind before I knew about this,"
she told her beau, Mr. Delaney.

"Why did we leave New York?" she would say to her
mother when she reminded them that the family roots
were all there beside the Hudson, not here beside the
Potomac.

Then she laughed and told her that they didn't leave
New York; New York had left them. So many things had
been left unanswered when her father set off for Cuba
and she was sixteen and he never returned.

She sat every morning before the mirror in her tiny
bedroom on Fourteenth Street, and there came a day
when she admitted that her face was telling a story that
didn't please her.

She was only thirty-one, but the features she traced

[47]

gently on the mirror before touching her icy temple with the same finger seemed not older but emptier, less legible than ten—even two—years before: like the blanched pages of a book after the words have disappeared.

She was a woman who dreamed a lot. If her soul was not different from her dreams, she could accept that both were instantaneous. Like a dream, her soul revealed itself in flashes. No, the soul isn't like that, she argued with herself in her dreams, the teachings of her religion filtering to the deepest center of the dream; the soul's not like that, she chastised herself for such thoughts; one's soul isn't something that belongs to the instant, it belongs to God, and is eternal.

She would awaken thinking of what she might have said but hadn't, of the errors and spectral hiatuses in her words and her waking acts, which pursued her throughout the night.

This was the realm of shadow, but light was a worse torture for her. In the darkness of dream, she sank into the hot tidewater summer, as she sank into the heat of her own sleeping body. Hers were the humidity of the banks of the Potomac and the wet and drooping vegetation of the city, domesticated in appearance only, in reality invading the farthest corners of forgotten gardens and cesspools, back yards shaded beneath dripping green roofs and carpeted with dead dogwood blossoms, and the sweet-sour smell of Negroes who drifted through a haze of dog days—sweaty bodies and lazily powdered faces.

Halfway between Washington and Mexico, she was to imagine that Washington had summer but Mexico had light. Suspended in her imagination between memory and visions of the future, both illuminations denuded the surrounding space. The Mexican sun could leave a landscape naked beneath its fire. The Potomac sun could become a luminous mist that devoured the contours of interiors, drawing rooms, bedchambers, the humid and hollow spaces of stinking cellars where cats crept to give birth to their litters, where the tired presence of rugs, furniture, and old clothes that lingered in Washington while people arrived and departed with their trunks, all joined together like latent, dispassionate ghosts amid a heavy smell of moss and mothballs.

At times she asked herself: "When was I most happy?"

She knew the answer: when her adored father had left and she felt she could be the responsible one. Now she was responsible. She had spent her childhood haunted by the brilliant yellow light she watched moving slowly from floor to floor in a recently constructed but already decaying mansion on Sixteenth Street. Hidden behind stubborn summer shrubs on a hill that plunged abruptly from an abandoned tennis court to a lawn covered with dead magnolias, she stared at the light as slowly it came and went, melting what must have been the soft interior, the buttery recesses behind the façade of carved stone, cut and assembled to resemble a fantasy of a Second Empire mansion, pompous and dank.

Who was carrying that lamp? Why did she feel that its light was calling to her? Who lived there? She never saw a face.

Now she stared at the light in the center of her mother's favorite table, a marble-topped table her father had used every night for the paperwork and the bills, and the family for eating, and now her mother used only for the latter. She stared at that domestic glow and realized that she had invested this simple household object, this everyday necessity, this green-shaded lamp with all the trembling imagination, all the passionate desire of the light she remembered from that humid summer mansion.

She reached out and took her mother's hand to tell her that she was leaving. Her mother already knew. She had opened the letter from the Mirandas, without asking her permission then or her pardon now.

Miss Harriet Winslow, 2400 Fourteenth Street . . .

"A cultivated young lady, but headstrong and fanciful . . ."

It didn't matter; she would never again listen to her mother.

She didn't realize it, but the daughter's promise of happiness and youth was evident only on the mother's face. The light worked this transference, this gift from the daughter. A light. Perhaps the same light she had followed like a ghost through the decaying mansion; that same light had come here, to this tiny apartment, to fulfill Miss Winslow's desire: that her mother reflect the brilliant light of her childhood; that the daughter no longer reflect the sorrowful shadow of the mother.

She dreamed: the light stopped at the foot of the service stairway beside the cellar that was the last and darkest labyrinth in the unserviceable shell of the intimidating and ephemeral façade of Washingtonian luxury and duty, the stark whiteness of the pantheon of the city, its black wells, and the smell became stronger. First she recognized half the smell, the smell of old mattresses and damp rugs, and then the other half, the smell of the couple lying there, the sour-sweet smell of love and blood, of moist armpits and genital spasms as her father possessed the solitary Negress who lived there, perhaps in the service of absent masters, perhaps she herself the repudiated lady of the house.

"Captain Winslow, I am very lonely. You may have me at your pleasure."

Mr. Delaney, who had been her beau for eight years, smelled like a laundry when he stole a kiss during their promenades through the summer evenings, and later, when it was all over, she saw that without his starched Arrow collar he was old and tired, and he said to her: Well, what can women be but sluts or virgins.

"Aren't you happy that I have chosen you as my ideal girl, Harriet?"

At dawn, General Arroyo informed the old gringo that their assignment was to clear out the countryside, mopping up what was left of the resistance in the region. Pockets of soldiers from the Federal army were trying to dig strongholds in the hills of the Sierra Madre, hoping to snipe at them and pin them down indefinitely, while the bulk of Villa's division was far to the south and had already taken the towns of the Laguna area. We have to move forward, the General said in a hard, dense voice, join Villa, but first we have to clean out the terrain here.

Then they weren't on their way to join Villa now? the old man asked uneasily. No, Arroyo replied. We'll meet General Villa later, wherever he decides, then together we'll ride against the city of Zacatecas and then Mexico City. That's the prize of the campaign. We have to get there before Obregón's and Carranza's men. Pancho Villa says that it's important for the Revolution.

We represent the people; they're nothing but a bunch of pretty boys. Villa is pressing on; we're to mop up the rearguard so they don't surprise us from behind, said Arroyo, now smiling. "We're what you call the 'floating brigade.' It isn't the most glorious job . . ."

The old man saw no reason to smile. The time had come and Pancho Villa was still a long way away. He said he would be ready in five minutes. He walked to the rear of the car, where the woman with the moon face lay asleep on the floor. She had given her bed to Miss Winslow. The Mexican woman awakened when the old man entered. He motioned her to be silent. She was not alarmed, and closed her eyes again. For a moment the old man stood gazing at the sleeping face of the beautiful American. He stroked her shining auburn hair; he pulled the serape over a small, round, half-exposed breast, and softly brushed the warm cheek with his lips. Maybe (or so the old gringo wished) the woman with the moon face understood his tenderness.

Dream is our personal myth, the old gringo said to himself as he kissed the sleeping Harriet, and he asked that her dream outlast the war, triumph over war itself, so that when he returned to her, dead or alive, she would welcome him in this uninterrupted dream that he—by the force of his desire and inducing by desire—was able to see and understand in the brief duration of a dream, and which later memory, or lack of memory, would restore as an elaborate plot peopled with details, structures, and incidents. Perhaps he wanted to invite her into his own dream; but his was a dream of death that could not be shared with anyone. However, as long as they both lived, no matter how great the distance between them, they could penetrate each other's dreams, share those dreams. He made a tremendous effort, as if this might be the last act of his life, and in an instant he dreamed with open eyes and clenched lips Harriet's entire dream, everything: the missing father; the mother, a prisoner of shadows; the transfer of the fixed light on the table and the fleeting light in the abandoned house.

"I am very lonely."

"You may have me at your pleasure."

". . . did you look at yourself in the mirror . . . ?"

"Did you see how they looked at themselves yesterday in the mirrors?" Arroyo asked as he mounted his black horse beside the gringo on his white mare. The old man stared from beneath white eyebrows. The battered Stetson did not conceal the icy-blue gaze. He nodded.

"They had never seen their whole bodies before. They didn't know their bodies were more than a piece of their imagination or a broken reflection in a river. Now they know."

"Is that why the ballroom was spared?"

"You're right, gringo. For that very reason."

"Why was everything else destroyed? What did you gain by that?"

"Look at those fields, Indiana General." Arroyo gestured with a swift, weary movement of his arm which pushed his sombrero onto his shoulders. "Not much grows here. Except memory and bitterness."

"And you believe that resentment and justice are the same thing, General," said the old man, smiling.

Arroyo's only reply was: "We're getting close to the foothills."

Then they were there. The old man saw a high sierra notched with yellow basalt. The mountains stood like ancient, exhausted beasts thrust from the womb of an infinitely indifferent and self-perpetuating range. The old man forced himself to remember that the Federal soldiers hidden there were not at all exhausted. He must be on the alert, just as when the Indiana Volunteers had helped Sherman wipe out what was left of Johnston's rebel army after the fall of Fayetteville. A terrible emptiness, almost an oblivion, filled the old gringo's head at that instant; then, a young man, he had wanted to fight on the side of the Blue, with the Union, against the Gray, the Rebels, simply because he had dreamed that his father was serving in the Army of the Confederacy, against Lincoln. He wanted what he had dreamed: the revolutionary drama of son against father.

"If they're going to attack, it's now or never," said the old man, swooping back to reality like a hawk on its prey. "We're in plain view now."

"If they attack, we'll know where they are," said Arroyo.

Bullets pierced the hard-crusted ground a dozen feet away.

"They're nervous." Arroyo grinned. "That's why they don't hit us."

He ordered a halt; everyone dismounted. Except the old man. He continued forward.

"Hey, Indiana General. Can't you handle your horse? I ordered a halt," Arroyo shouted.

And he continued to shout as the old man began to trot straight toward the rugged rocks from which the shots were being fired. "Hey, you fool gringo. Didn't you hear my order? Come back here, you old idiot!"

But the old man continued straight on while the burst of machine-gun fire passed over his head, aimed at Arroyo and his men, not at the mirage of a white knight on a white horse, so visible he seemed invisible, trotting forward as if unaware of the fire, readying himself, loosening his lasso from the pommel of his saddle. Arroyo and his men fell flat against the ground, more frightened for the old gringo than for themselves or for the Federales lying in ambush. There on their bellies, they realized that the Federal soldiers had miscalculated, that the machine-gun fire was neither reaching them nor hitting the old man. But any minute now they would realize their error. And then, adios, old gringo, murmured Arroyo, his breast pressed to the ground.

They saw him coming, but the truth was, they didn't believe it. The old man understood what was happening as soon as he saw their astonished faces. He wasn't like them, he was an avenging white devil, he had eyes that only God in the churches had, his Stetson flew off and they saw revealed the image of God the Father. He was in their imaginations; he wasn't real. The handful of Federal soldiers were so stunned by the vision that they were slow to recover their senses, clumsy in exchanging machine gun for rifles, never realizing that behind them a Confederate commander on horseback, his sword unsheathed, was urging them on to victory, and that it was toward this horseman, flashing his anger from the mountaintop, the gringo rode, not toward them, their machine gun lost now, lassoed and tumbled out of sight, and then the wrinkled, sere apparition fired on the four sharpshooters and they lay dead beneath the burning sun, flat on the fiery rocks, their faces hot in death, their feet digging into the surprised dust as if wanting to run toward their deaths, challenge death to a footrace. A single shout burst from the rebel force, but the gringo did not hear it; he was still firing upward, toward the peaks where first rode, and then fell, the horseman dressed in gray, but whiter than he, hurtling through the air: the horseman in the sky.

Everyone ran to the old gringo, to stop him, to congratulate him, brushing dirt and burrs from their chests, but he was still firing toward the cliff, toward the sky, oblivious to the shouting of his comrades, who could not know that for him a story was becoming a ghostly reality, a story in which he was a Union Army lookout who had fallen asleep for a minute and then was awakened by a voice never heard by mortal, the voice of his Southern father, riding a white horse along the ridge of a high cliff: Do what you conceive to be your duty, sir.

"I have killed my father."

"You are a brave man, Indiana General," Arroyo said.

The old man stared long and hard into the General's eyes, thinking that he could tell him many things. But no one would be interested in his story. Except maybe Harriet Winslow. And even she, who had lost a father in a war, would take such a story too literally. For the old gringo, dazed by the fragility of the planet that separates reality from fiction, the problem was different: journalist or writer, he was still pursued by alternatives. It was not the same, but he must shake all the options from his head. He could not go on believing that he was going to live, to work, to choose between the news directed to Hearst and his readers and the fiction directed to the father and the woman; nor was it possible for him to continue to sacrifice the latter to the former. There was only one option, and that is why his only response to Arroyo was: "It's not difficult to be brave when you're not afraid to die."

But Arroyo knew that the mountains were already

shouting it, from chasm to peak, from cave to canyon, across barrancas and bone-dry creeks: A brave man has come here, a brave man is among us, a brave man has set foot on our stones.

9 But the desert forgets us, the old gringo told himself that morning. At the same moment, Arroyo, staring at the sky, was thinking that everything had a home except him and the clouds. Harriet Winslow awoke saying the word *"mañana,"* accusing it of having prolonged her sleep only to awaken her with an uncomfortable sensation of having procrastinated in some duty. The old man's question (Had she looked at herself in the ballroom mirror?) kept returning, and Harriet wondered, and why not?—even though mirrors were beginning to tell her a story that didn't please her. Maybe last night the old man had wanted to ask her whether she had seen something different in the hacienda mirrors, or what she always saw.

"Your soul is no different from your dreams. Both are instantaneous."

"The soul does not belong to the instant. It isn't a dream. It is eternal."

That is why the morning of the skirmish that was still unknown to her, she walked with a firm step to the village adjoining the hacienda, fresh and brisk in her shirtwaist and tie, full pleated wool skirt and high-button boots, the auburn hair pulled back into a bun, murmuring: First things first—forgetting that when she had awakened she had felt undecided about what she could have said but hadn't in her encounters with the General and the old man, reconstructing the spectral hiatuses in her waking speech and actions that pursued her throughout the night. Daily activity was all the more important for that very fact, intending first to incorporate, but later destroy, the nocturnal attacks on the instant. But she would sleep again, she would dream again: dream's interruption of the minute hand that daily grinds away true internal time in the mill of activity merely emphasizes, and intensifies, the world of the eternal instant that would return by night, while she slept and dreamed alone.

When the detachment returned at dusk, Arroyo found the men who had remained behind busy among the ruins of the hacienda, the women preparing great pails of whitewash, and the children seated around Miss Winslow in the ballroom that had been spared from destruction. The children were avoiding looking at themselves in the mirrors. The teacher had lectured strongly against vanity: This ballroom is a temptation sent to test our Christian humility, a ballroom filled with the sin of presumption.

"Did you look at yourselves in the mirrors when you entered the ballroom?"

She had learned some Spanish in her Washington normal school, and could speak with firmness, even correctness, when she was not frightened as she had been the night before: Presumption, Vanity, the Devil, Sin. The children thought that the nice American lady's lesson was not very different from the sermons of the parish priest here on the hacienda, except that in the chapel there were prettier and more entertaining things to look at while the priest was talking. Miss Harriet Winslow questioned them and found them bright and forthcoming. But have you visited the pretty little chapel, señorita?

"Did you see anything different from what you saw in Washington; is the image always the same?"

When Tomás Arroyo, whip in hand, marched into the ballroom, Harriet Winslow met his eyes squarely. She saw his contained fury and she gloried in it. Who had given the señorita permission to rebuild the hacienda? Why had she commandeered his men?

"So that people can have a roof over their heads," Miss Winslow answered simply. "Not everyone can sleep in a Pullman car designed for the Vanderbilts."

The General stared at her through eyes narrower than ever. "I want this place to be a ruin. I want the house of the Mirandas to *remain* a ruin."

"You are mad, sir," said Harriet, with all the serenity she could muster.

His heels rang threateningly as he walked toward her, but he stopped short of touching her. "Arroyo. My name is General Arroyo."

He waited, but she did not respond. He shouted: "You understand now? No one touches this place. It stays the way it is."

"You are mad, sir."

Now there was insult in Harriet's voice. He seized her violently by the arm and she stifled a moan.

"Why don't you say it? General. General Arroyo!"

"Let me go!"

"Answer me, I tell you!"

"Because you are not a general. No one appointed you. I am sure you named yourself."

"Come with me."

He dragged her out into the late evening. The old gringo was drinking a glass of tequila in the General's car when he heard the commotion and went out on the platform. He saw them clearly, facing the setting sun: she, tall and slim; he, short for a man but muscular, his manliness compensating for what the American woman took from him in height or manners or whatever you might call what he now feared and desired from her. These were the old man's thoughts as he watched and listened on the day of his heroic action, a day when he had not wanted to sit down and write to compensate for his physical exertion and so was getting drunk and praying that this day would soon end and the next day come, the day that might be the day of his death. But he knew that the prize, as always, went not to the brave but to the young: dying or writing, loving or dying. He closed his eyes in fear: what he had seen in the distance were a son and a daughter; he opaque, she transparent, but both born of the seed of the imagination called poetry and love. He was fearful because he did not want love again in his life.

Look, Arroyo said to Miss Winslow, as he had to the old gringo that morning, look at this land. She saw a dry, ugly, but beautifully dramatic world, strong, devoid of any generosity, alien to fruit easy for the picking: she saw a land whose scanty fruits had to be born of a dead womb, like a child that goes on living and fighting to be born from its dead mother's womb.

Both Harriet and the old man were thinking of other, more opulent lands, of fertile, long, lazy rivers, of the splendor of waving wheat fields on land stretching flat as a tablecloth toward smoky blue mountains and gently rolling mountainsides covered with forests. The rivers:

they thought especially of the rivers of the North, a litany that rolled from their tongues like a current of lost pleasures in that dry and thirsty Mexican evening. Hudson, the old man said; Ohio, Mississippi, she answered from the distance; Missouri, Potomac, Delaware, the old gringo concluded: the good, green waters.

What was it the old gringo had said to Miss Harriet last night? That she had come as a schoolmistress to a hacienda she had never seen, which no longer existed, to teach English to children she didn't know, or know anything about, even if they did exist.

"They got bored," Arroyo said, his words heavy and dry in this land without rivers.

They got bored: the masters of the hacienda came here from time to time, only as a vacation. An overseer administered everything for them. These were no longer the times of the resident landowner who kept a close eye on the cattle and weighed every quintal of grain. When these owners came, they got bored and drank cognac. They fought the young bulls. They also went galloping through the tilled fields, terrifying the peons bent over their humble Chihuahua crops, beans, wild lettuce, spindly wheat; they beat the backs of the weakest men with the flat of a machete, and they lassoed the weakest women and then raped them in the hacienda stables while the mothers of the young gentlemen pretended not to hear the screams of our mothers and the fathers of the young gentlemen drank cognac in the library and said, They're young, this is the age for sowing their wild oats, better now than later. They'll settle down. We did the same.

Now Arroyo wasn't pointing toward the accursed land. Now he was forcing Harriet to look at the charred ruins of the hacienda. She did not physically resist because she did not mentally resist. She was conceding to Arroyo what was Arroyo's, the old man told himself, drunk from his military exploits, the resurrected literary worm, his desire for death, his fear of a disfiguring death: dogs, knives, the memory of another's pain when it becomes one's own; his fear of dying choked by asthma; his desire to die by another's hand. All these thoughts at the same time: "I want to be a good-looking corpse."

"I am the son of some man's wild oats, the son of chance and misfortune, señorita. No one protected my mother. She was a young girl. She had no husband, no one to defend her. I was born to defend her. Look, miss. No one defended anyone here. Not even the bulls. Castrating bulls, yes, that was more exciting than fucking the local girls. I saw their eyes shine as they cut off their balls, shouting, Ox, ox, sexless cows!"

He was gripping Harriet's shoulders but she did not resist because she knew that Arroyo never said such things to anyone and maybe she understood that what Arroyo was saying was true only because he did not know the world. "Who named me general? I tell you who. Misfortune named me general. Silence named me general, having to hold my tongue. Here they killed you if you made any noise in bed. If a man and a woman moaned while they were in bed together, they were whipped. That was lack of respect for the Mirandas. They were decent people. We made love and we gave birth without a sound, señorita. Instead of a voice, I have a paper. Ask your friend the old man. Is he taking good care of you?" Arroyo asked as, without respect to the conventions, he passed abruptly from drama to comedy.

"Revenge," said Harriet, ignoring him. "Revenge is your motive. This is your monument to revenge, but also to your scorn for your own people. You can't eat revenge, General."

"Ask them, then," said Arroyo, gesturing toward his people.

(The brave Inocencio Mansalvo told her: "Me, I don't like the land, señorita. I would lie if I told you I did. I do not want to spend my life stooped over in the fields. I want the haciendas to be destroyed; I want all the people who work the land to be free, so we can work wherever we want, in the city or in the North—in your country, señorita. And if it is not to be so, I will go on fighting forever. No more stooping for me; I want men to look me in the face.")

(La Garduña told her: "My papa was a hardheaded man. He got it in his head to guard the worthless bit of land we'd moved onto, but armed men from the hacienda came and killed my papa and my mama, who was going to have a little brother or a little sister, who will ever know . . . ? I was just a tiny kid and I hid under a cooking pot. Some neighbors sent me to Durango to live with my old-maid aunt, doña Josefa Arreola. One day the Revolution whirled by and a boy caught my eye, a boy who moved and seemed to call to me . . . Ay, my poor papa, ay, my poor mama, ay, the poor little dead angel . . .")

(Colonel García told her: "They were smothering us in these provincial towns, Señorita Winslow. The very air was draped in mourning. Sometimes here you see the lowest people, former rustlers, peons who had nothing, or those who just plain like trouble. But look at me. I

[63]

am the son of a merchant. Ask yourself how many like me have taken up arms to support the Revolution, and I am talking about professional people, writers, teachers, small manufacturers. We can govern ourselves, I assure you, señorita. We are tired of a world ruled by the caciques, the Church, and the strutting aristocrats we've always had here. You don't think we are capable, then? Or do you fear the violence that has to precede freedom?")

"Ask them, then," said Arroyo, gesturing toward his people. He turned his back to Harriet, walking away proudly, his head to one side.

From the platform of the Pullman car, the old man watched and listened and imagined.

"What is the strongest pretext for loving? Is it different from the pretext for acting?"

Anyway, he understood that Arroyo was taking this opportunity to show him "what he had in his head" in place of an alphabet.

 He was beginning to feel the alcohol, but he met her at the platform of the car and offered her his arm like a gentleman of the old school, all his conflicts resolved into this reality: a young and beautiful woman in a pleasant social situation far removed from any decisions; life, after all ...

She accepted a small glass of tequila.

"So!" Harriet Winslow sighed, playing the role of a

North American woman with the prospect of a comforting glass at dusk with a fellow American. "It isn't easy, you know, to leave New York behind. Washington really isn't a city, it's a place of passage. The principal actors change so often." She laughed quietly, and the old man had to wonder whether this conversation was taking place at nightfall in a savage Mexican desert.

"Why did you leave New York?" he asked.

"Why did New York leave us?" Her quiet laughter expressed her pleasure, and the old man told himself that Harriet's drink must be taking effect more quickly than his, with a more dizzying result. All he wanted to ask, yet again, was: As you entered the ballroom, did you look at yourself in the mirrors?

But with a swift glance at the woman who only a few moments earlier had in effect been in the arms of a young foreigner, he realized that she would prefer not to talk about that; neither, however, did she want to appear gauche and ask him about his own life. That morning she had seen the old man's open suitcase, two books in English, both by the same author, and a copy of the *Quixote*; and now, beside his glass, she saw some pages of manuscript and a stubby pencil. It was easier for both of them to talk about her, about her past. The old man had fought today; he could have died. She sipped her drink and said to him, wordlessly, I know you fought today, the excitement is in your face; I would not deny you a little candor, even a little warmth. That's why she chose to speak about herself and answer the old man's insistent question obliquely: "So many things were left unanswered when my father went to Cuba. I was sixteen, and he never returned."

[65]

She told him that her family history was bizarre, you would think she had invented it, especially "when I tell it to you here." In the 1840s, her great-uncle had been one of the richest men in New York. He had a son of whom he was very proud, and he sent him off to Europe to become a man. In addition, as a sign of fatherly confidence, he charged him with buying some Old Masters. Instead, "my marvelous Uncle Lewis" had bought paintings no one appreciated then: Giottos, and primitive masters. "You know what? My Great-uncle Halston disinherited him! He thought his son had made a fool of him by buying such horrible and crude paintings, totally unsuitable to be shown to ladies and gentlemen in the drawing room of a mansion on the shores of Long Island Sound.

"He left all his money to his two daughters, and as a kind of joke, he left Lewis the paintings, which he considered worthless. Uncle Lewis kept the pictures and died in poverty. A maiden aunt kept them in her attic, and when my own grandmother inherited them, she gave them to somebody. When they were finally auctioned twenty years ago, they brought five million dollars. Uncle Lewis had paid five thousand. But for us, it was too late."

She raised her glass and said to the old gringo: Can you imagine? And he said yes, he could imagine a young girl's dreams of being wealthy in New York at the beginning of the century, when life was sweet there; instead, "having to wait, as her mother had also had to wait, it wasn't easy, no, it wasn't easy," because they weren't accustomed to accepting charity, in whatever form; suitors did not flock around a girl without a dowry, the daughter of a minor officer fallen in the Cuban campaign, the daughter of a widow of an army captain, studying at a normal school in Washington, D.C., to be near God knows what and . . .

"Well, then . . . What about you? That's the end of my story."

"Imagine . . ."

"Yes," she said, "yes," and again she glanced at the scribbled sheets of paper, the stubby pencil. "We studied literature in school, you know, sir. It is admirable that you brought Cervantes's book to Mexico."

"I've never read it," said the old gringo. "I thought here . . ."

"It is never too late to read the classics." This time Harriet held out her glass and the gringo filled it before serving himself his fourth, his fifth . . . "Or our contemporaries. I see also that you brought two books by a living American author . . ."

"Don't read them," said the old man, wiping the sting of the tequila from his mustache. "They are very bitter books, the devil's dictionaries . . ."

"And you?" she insisted, as he had insisted: Had she seen herself in the mirrors when she entered the ballroom? What story did the mirrors tell her?

He? Did she think he was going to tell her everything he was feeling? I came here to die, I am a writer, I want to be a good-looking corpse, I cannot bear to cut myself when I am shaving, I live in terror that a rabid dog will bite me and I will die disfigured, I am not afraid of bullets, I want to read *Don Quixote* before I die, to be a gringo in Mexico is one way of dying, I am . . .

"A bitter old man. Pay no attention to me. Coincidence brought us together. If I hadn't met you, Miss

Harriet, I'm sure I would have come across one of the American newspapermen trailing along after Villa. I wouldn't have to tell him my story. He would know it."

"But I don't," said Harriet Winslow. "And I have been candid with you. A bitter old man, you say?"

"Old Bitters. A contemptible, muckraking reporter at the service of a baron of the press as corrupt as any I denounced in his name. But I was pure, Miss Harriet, do you believe me? Pure, but bitter. I attacked the honor and dishonor of all men, without distinction. In my time, I was feared and hated. Here, have another, and don't look at me like that. You asked me to be frank. I am going to be. Being frank is what I do best."

"I'm not sure, truthfully, that . . ."

"No, no, no!" the old gringo said, dogmatically. "You know why you have to listen to me today."

"Tomorrow . . . I know your name."

The old man grimaced ironically. "My name was synonymous with coldness, with anti-sentimentality. I was the devil's disciple, except that I wouldn't have accepted even the devil as master. Much less God, whom I defamed with something worse than blasphemy: a curse on everything He had wrought."

She attempted a graceful diversion: she was a Methodist, he was dreaming, give her a minute, she wanted to imagine it; but he would brook no trick, no distraction. He had invented a new decalogue, the old man said abruptly: "Adore no images save those the coinage of the country shows; Kill not, for death liberates your foe from persecution's constant woe; To steal were folly, for 'tis plain, in cheating there is greater gain; Honor thy parents, and perchance their wills thy fortune may advance."

"So I invented myself a new family, the family of my imagination, through my Club of Parenticides, the target of destruction. Good God. Why, I detected signs of cannibalism even at my mother's breast, and I urged lovers to bite one another when they kissed, yes, nip, bite, animals, devour another, bite and . . . ha!"

He leaped from his chair, scattering the pencil and papers precariously balanced on the armrest of the chair where he had been sitting; from the platform they saw the desert night renewing its kinship with the vanished sea. In the distance, the bald harsh mountains were the color of the pyramids. Birds flew by, trailing the sound of dry, rustling grass.

"Oh, I had my moment of glory," the old man said, laughing sarcastically; on his knees, picking up the scattered writing utensils. "I became so much a nemesis for California's great corruptor and defaulter that finally he invited me to visit him in his office, and tried to bribe me. 'Oh, no,' I said, 'you can't corrupt me.' He laughed, Miss Winslow, as I am laughing now, and said, 'Every man has his price.' I answered, 'You're right. Write me a check for seventy-five million dollars.' 'In your name or made out to the bearer?' asked Leland Stanford, checkbook open and pen in hand, mocking me with something worse than mockery, the complicity in his mouse-gray eyes. 'No,' I said, 'in the name of the Treasury of the United States, and for the exact amount of the public lands you stole!' Miss Winslow, you never saw a face like Stanford's when I told him that. Ha!"

The old man enjoyed his audacity more now than when he had been in Stanford's office. Then, he'd had to keep a wooden face, and now he could enjoy it; the memory was better than the fact; oh, could he laugh

[69]

now! So tomorrow he would die? It's true, you know, he said, drying tears of laughter with the skirt of a tasseled red tablecloth; a muckraking reporter needs a robber baron as God needs Satan or a flower needs manure; without the low, what can you compare glory to?

He did not speak for a moment, and she shared the silence. He was remembering his ride through the mountains several days before, and even now recalled the powerful breath of creation that blows across the Sierra Madre.

"I should have accepted Stanford's offer and thrown Hearst's job in his face, instead of going on scrimping, denying comfort to my wife and children, and then compounding my guilt by squandering what little I'd saved in those damned bars in San Francisco where all good Californians got together to stare off into the sea, so we could tell ourselves: The frontier's gone, boys; the continent's dead; Manifest Destiny's gone to hell in a hand basket; so where are we to find adventure? In a desert mirage?"

And after another drink: "No more West, boys, except in the blurry frontier of an empty whiskey glass."

Harriet took the old man's shaking hand and asked him whether he was sure he wanted to go on, wasn't what he'd already said defeat enough, and an atonement in memory? But he said no, it wasn't an atonement because he'd kept trying to justify himself; he wasn't responsible.

"I saw myself as a kind of avenging angel, you see. I was the bitter and sardonic disciple of the devil because I was trying to be as sanctimonious as the people I scorned. You surely understand, you a Methodist, I a Calvinist; each of us trying to be more virtuous than the

[70]

next, to win the race to see who is the most puritanical, but, in the process, offending whoever is closest to us— for you will see, Miss Harriet, that in fact the only power I had was over my wife and children, not my readers, they were as smug as I, or Hearst; they were every one firmly on the side of morality and rectitude and indignation; each of them said: I'm not the person you're denouncing, no, that's my despicable brother, that other reader. No, I had no power over the targets of my journalistic rage and even less over the men who manipulated my humor and my anger to their own ends. Long live democracy!"

She did not release his hand. (She sits alone and remembers.) Why, she wondered, should she have to choose between those here who sought the curse of death but nevertheless lived their final moments seeking understanding and those who conceived of death as a gift of life, but turned away from the gift, refusing to accept it. She stroked the old man's rough hand with its heavy wedding band. All she could say, with an awakening of affection, was: "Then how is it you know what it means to be defeated?" She spoke in English, but with an imperceptible change of tone, a movement toward the affectionate familiarity expressed in the Spanish "tú." The old man was too wrapped up in himself, in his memory, to notice, murmuring that one day the bitter old cynic discovered he was as sentimental as the people he had scorned: an old man drowning in nostalgia and memories of love and laughter.

"I couldn't bear the pain of those I loved. And I couldn't bear myself for being a sentimental fool when misfortune tapped my shoulder."

He pressed Harriet Winslow's hands as the passing

clouds of night vainly sought their mirror in the desert and continued on their errant destiny. He wasn't, he swore to Miss Harriet, asking her to share his misfortune; it was just that tomorrow, maybe . . . She understood; she was the only one who could understand, and they both felt a little happiness.

"But I have no misfortune to share." Miss Winslow spoke abruptly, coldly. "I have suffered only humiliation, and I scorn gossip."

He was not really listening now, nor was he able to measure the many shadings of her moods, capricious, willful, dignified, weak. But he continued to hold her hands in his.

"I only wanted to tell you that you must understand the defeat of a man who believed he was master of his fate, who even believed he could shape the destinies of others through a journalism of accusation and satire, I, who stoutly insisted I was the friend of Truth, not of Plato, while my lord and master of the press cannibalized my anger for the greater glory of his political interests and his massive circulation and his massive bank accounts. Oh, what a fool I was, Miss Harriet! But that's what they paid me for, for being the idiot, the buffoon, in the pay of my lord and master on this earth."

He lightly embraced Harriet, burying his face in that hair that was the living answer to the desert, thinking only that it was the stirring of physical love that moved him to go on living, the nearness of another body, not the hated sentiment and compassion, hoping that she would understand or accept such a distinction, accept in her father's name the old gringo she wanted to see and listen to, not as a journalist, but as a military man lost in action, lost in the desert with no comfort but hers, his compatriot imbued with notions of military honor and of the succor due compatriots in a foreign land. My own son died twice, he told her, first as an alcoholic and then as a suicide, after reading me and telling me, Old man, you have written the blueprint for my death, oh, beloved old man.

"One afflicted with a painful or loathsome disease, one who is a heavy burden to those he cares for, one threatened with insanity, one without property, employment, or hope, one who has disgraced himself, one irreclaimably addicted to drunkenness! Why honor a valiant soldier or fireman and not the dutiful suicide?

"You see, Harriet," he said to her, as if he were speaking to the dead stars, not into the warm, moist ear so close to his lips, as if the woman's arms were not pressing him to her breast, "they weren't really against me, they were against the life I lived. The man who was my older son decided to die in the horrible world I had written for him. And the man who was my younger son decided to die by proving to me he had the courage to die for courage."

He laughed aloud. "I think my sons killed themselves so I wouldn't ridicule them in the newspapers of my boss William Randolph Hearst."

"And your wife?"

The old gringo's eyes followed the line of salt cedars bordering the meager river. Those thirsty, luxuriant shrubs hoarded the scarce water only to turn it bitter, salty, useless for any purpose. She died lonely and filled with bitterness; she died of a deep and consuming illness, the feeling that she had wasted a lifetime in the thousand sad recriminations of two people who go for days without speaking, without even looking at one another;

the unsufferable encounters of two blinded animals in a black cave.

"Only death can compensate for so much vindictive bile, the demands for silence, genius at work, and then, where is the proof of the much-vaunted talent?" the old man asked, returning to reality, aware of the pain in his head, moving away from Harriet Winslow as the sinner moves from the confessional and looks for a floor where he may kneel to carry out his penance. The old gringo tried to pierce the desert's inky blackness, to imagine the creosote bushes that grow there, maintaining their distance from other plants because their poisonous roots kill anything that grows near them. So he moved away from Harriet Winslow.

"And your daughter?" she asked in a voice that trembled for the first time, and immediately cursed that betrayal of feeling.

"My daughter swore never to see me again," he replied, struggling to compose himself, his nervous hands vainly searching for a glass or a piece of paper. "She told me: I shall die without ever seeing you again, and I hope you die before you learn how much you will miss me. But I doubt that, Miss Harriet, I doubt it because in her eyes I saw the burning hope that I would remember all the little things that, in spite of everything, held us together so many years. Was it like that with the three of you, Miss Harriet, you and your father and mother?"

She didn't answer. She wanted to hear the end. She didn't want the old man to gaze sightlessly again into the desert night, looking for impossible analogies. (She still sits and remembers. She wanted the old man to finish, so she would never have to begin.) She knew that the tragicomic story of her Great-uncle Halston and the Italian paintings was not enough to pay for the gift her old compatriot the writer had given her in the story of his life.

"And your daughter?"

"Do you remember the many little pleasures shared between a father and a daughter, and then the enormous grief of understanding that all that is gone forever?"

"And your daughter?" Harriet Winslow almost screamed, but with a stubborn, controlled coldness.

"She told me she would never forgive the mortal pain she suffered before the bodies of her two brothers. You killed them both, she told me, both of them."

"And your country?" Harriet rose now with anger, disguising her fear of not continuing alone, I must answer the old man, and your country? And he fell into the trap. I mocked that, too, of course; did she want to know that he had also scoffed at the meaning of national honor, of patriotic duty, of loyalty to the flag? Why, yes, even that, that is why his family feared him, he had mocked God, his Homeland, Money; for God's sake, then: when would it be their turn? They must have asked themselves that, when will it be our turn? when will our accursed father turn against us, judging us, telling us you're no exception, you prove the rule, and you, too, wife, and you, my beautiful daughter, and you, my sons, you are all a part of the ludicrous filth, the farts of God, we call humanity.

"I shall destroy you all with my ridicule. I shall bury you all beneath my poisonous laughter. I shall laugh at you as I laugh at the United States, at its ridiculous army and flag," the old man said breathlessly, choking with asthma.

My country 'tis of thee,
Sweet land of felony . . .

Harriet made no move to help him. She merely watched him choking, bent over like a folded shaving knife in the little wicker chair on the platform of the railroad car.

"I tell you, I respect the army." Harriet spoke as neutrally as she could, trying not to sound argumentative, because at least the old man had not lied to her.

"Because the army intervened between you and the poorhouse?" The old man wheezed, his eyes shining with tears, but determined to die on the bitter edge of mockery, choked by his own laughter. "Then it *was* the poorhouse. I'm sorry."

"I am not ashamed of our nation or our forefathers. I told you, my father died in Cuba, missing in action . . ."

"I'm sorry." The old man coughed, who minutes before had stroked the hands and buried his face in the auburn hair of a beautiful woman. "Open your eyes, Miss Harriet, and remember how we killed our Redskins and never had the courage to fornicate with the squaws and at least create a half-breed nation. We are caught in the business of forever killing people whose skin is of a different color. Mexico is the proof of what we could have been, so keep your eyes wide open."

"I see now. You are ashamed that you were open and human with me. You cannot bear the pain of those you loved."

The old gringo had written at length about his father. He had been a soldier, he had fought against naked savages and followed the flag of his country into the capital of a civilized race to the far south. But he didn't say that to her now; he didn't want to share anything more with her, or let her believe she was right about anything. He wondered whether this was all they had in common, war between brothers, wars against the "savages," wars against the weak and the foreign. He said nothing because he wanted to hope that something more, someone else, could still unite them, without her having to depend on him to be able to understand anything here. He would not soon forget the smell of her hair, the softness of her skin, her desirable hands. Maybe it was already too late: she had disappeared and he was alone facing the desert. Maybe he could visit her dreams. Maybe the woman who entered the ballroom the previous evening had not looked at herself, but had dreamed herself.

"They live a life we don't understand," said Inocencio Mansalvo. "Do they want to know more about our lives? Well, they will have to make them up, because we're still nothing and nobody."

General Arroyo told him that the Federal army, whose officers had studied in the French Military Academy, were waiting to engage them in formal combat, where they knew all the rules and the guerrillas didn't. "They are like virgins," said the young Mexican general, hard and dark as a glazed pot. "They want to follow the rules. I want to make them."

Had the old man heard what Señorita Winslow said last night? Had he heard what the people in the camp and from the hacienda were saying? Why couldn't the people govern themselves here in their own land: was that too much to dream? He clenched his jaws and said that maybe he and the señorita wanted the same thing, but she didn't want the violence that had to come first. He knew, though, Arroyo told the old gringo, he knew there had to be a new violence to end the old violence. Colonel Frutos García was a man who had read many books, and he said that without the new violence the old violence would go on forever, just the same, yes? Isn't that right, Indiana General?

For a long time the old man's eyes were fixed on the rugged trail they were following. Then he said that he understood what the General was trying to say, and he was grateful he had the words to say it. They were the words of a man, he said, and he thanked him for them because they bound him once again to other men, after he had made a profession of refusing solidarity—or any other virtue, why deny it, said the old gringo, hoping his hat would hide his smile.

They rode alone in silence toward the rendezvous. The old man thought, here he was in Mexico looking for death, and what did he know about the country? Last night, remembering that his father had participated in the invasion of 1847 and the occupation of Mexico City, he had quoted a sentence to the desert. Then he remembered that Hearst had sent a radical from his newspaper to report on Porfirio Díaz's Mexico and that the journalist had returned and said that Díaz was a tyrant who did not tolerate opposition and had frozen the country in a kind of servitude where the people were the servants of large landowners, the army, and foreigners. Hearst did not allow the story to be published: this powerful baron of the press had his radical and his tyrant; he liked them both, but he defended only the tyrant. So what if Díaz was a tyrant, he was the father of his people, a weak people who needed a strict father, Hearst had said, picking his way through the many treasures stacked amid boxes and sawdust and nails in the storerooms of his mansion.

"There is something you don't know," Arroyo said to the gringo. "When he was young, Porfirio Díaz was a brave soldier, the best guerrilla ever to fight against Maximilian and the French Army. When he was my age, he was a poor general like me, a revolutionary and a patriot. I bet you didn't know that!"

No, the gringo said, he hadn't known. He only knew that fathers appear to their sons at night and on horseback, outlined atop a high cliff, serving in the opposing army and bidding their sons: "Carry out your duty. Fire upon your fathers."

At this early desert hour the mountains seem to await the horsemen in every ravine, as if they were in truth horsemen of the sky; horizons disappear, and at the bend of a trail the mountain waits to spring on the rider like a ravening beast. In the desert, as the saying goes, two or three times a day you may look upon God's face. The old gringo feared a similar fate: seeing the face of his father; he was riding beside a son: Arroyo, the son of misfortune.

How subtle, the old gringo thought in that early hour, is the knowledge a father inherits from all his fathers and transmits to all his sons. He thought he knew this better than many, he said, speaking aloud now, not

knowing or caring whether Arroyo understood him: he
had to say it. He had been accused of fictional parenti-
cide, but not at the level of an entire people who lived
their history as a series of murders of old, no longer
useful, fathers. No, he knew what he was talking about;
even when he had so rapidly diagnosed and filed Miss
Winslow; he, the old man, the bitter jester who had
come to the end of his personal tether, the son of a hell-
fire Calvinist who also loved Byron, and who one day
feared his son would try to kill him as he slept, this son,
first overly imaginative and then hideously in contempt
of everything the family had inherited and naturally
hoped to prolong: parsimony, thrift, faith, love for one's
parents, a sense of responsibility. He looked at Arroyo,
who hadn't even heard him. The gringo thought how
ironic it was that he the son was traveling the same road
his father had followed in 1847.

"Look at the cattle," said Arroyo. "They're dying."

But the old man did not see the pasturelands of the
Mirandas; his eyes were blinded by a fog of self-contra-
diction as he thought of his dead father alive in Mexico
in a different century, asking the son whether—knowing
the accusations that had been made, the resentment
Mexico felt toward all Americans—he hadn't come here
for that very reason but, further adding his injury to the
insult of his homeland, to provoke Mexico to do for him
what he didn't dare do for himself, out of some sense
of honor and self-respect: not die, as he had thought, but
succumb to love for a young girl.

"Would you fall in love with a young girl, if you were
my age?" the old gringo asked jokingly.

"You should make it your job to take care of young
girls and see that nothing bad happens to them." Arroyo

smiled in return. "I already told you, see that this one is well protected and think of her as your own daughter."

"That's what I meant, General."

"That's all you meant, Indiana General?"

The old man smiled. Sometime he had to begin to do what he pleased; now was as good a time as any. Who could say that it wouldn't be Arroyo, not he, who was the most distinguished dead man this day?

"Yes, I've been thinking about your fate, General Arroyo."

Arroyo laughed. "My fate is my business."

"Let's just imagine that it will be the same as that of Porfirio Díaz," the gringo continued, undaunted. "Let me imagine for you a future of power, force, oppression, pride, indifference. Do you know any revolution that has escaped that fate, General? Why would the children of their mother the Revolution escape her fate?"

"You tell me. Has any country avoided those evils— even yours, gringo?" Arroyo asked, leaning forward in the saddle, and calm as the old gringo himself.

"No, I'm talking about your personal destiny, not the destiny of any country, General Arroyo. The only way you will escape corruption is to die young."

Contrary to the old man's intentions, his words seemed to please Arroyo. "You guessed my thoughts, Indiana General. I have never dreamed of myself as an old man. And you? Why didn't you die in time, you old bastard?" Arroyo laughed aloud.

The old gringo surrendered before the Mexican's humor, and said only what he sometimes said to the stars: This land . . . He had never seen it before; he had attacked it by orders of his boss Hearst, who had enormous investments in ranches and other property and feared the Revolution; but as he couldn't say, Go protect my property, he had to say, Go protect our lives, there are North American citizens in danger, intervene!

"Ah, these gringos," Arroyo exclaimed with biting sarcasm. "Didn't I tell you they all talk Chinese . . . You have no idea what we have a right to, you don't know anything about it! Anyone who is born with the stink of a straw roof in his nose has a right to anything, Indiana General, anything!"

There was no time to answer, or even think, because they had come to a steep, stony slope where a lookout was waiting for the General. He said that everything was ready, as the General had ordered.

Arroyo looked directly at the old man and told him that now he had to make a choice. They were going to play a trick on the Federal troops. Half of the rebels were to march across the plain to meet the regular army the way they liked, head on, as they had been taught in their academies. The other half would fan out through the mountains behind the Federal lines, keeping out of sight, blending into the mountains like lizards, you can bet your old ass, Arroyo guffawed sourly, and while the Federales were fighting their formal battle with the decoy guerrilla troops on the plain, they would cut their supply lines, attack them from the rear, and catch them like rats in a trap.

"You say I have to make a choice?"

"Yes, Indiana General. Where do you want to be?"

"On the plain," the old man replied, without an instant's hesitation. "Not for the glory, you understand, but for the danger."

"Oh, so you think guerrilla fighting is not so dangerous?"

[82]

"It's more dangerous, but less glorious. You fight under cover, General Arroyo. And you are forced to improvise. If I understand my role clearly, on the plain all I have to do is march straight ahead while looking brave, trying not to think about the fact that a cannonball might blow off my head. Let me do that."

The Asiatic mask of Arroyo's face betrayed no emotion. He spurred his horse along the rocky trail, and the lookout led the old man to join the troops on the plain. He looked at the soldiers' faces, as impassive as Arroyo's. Were they thinking the same things he was thinking? Did they know? Were they brave, as he was, or were they merely following orders, convinced they would be lucky? Would they fight with conviction on the stage set their remarkable General Arroyo had constructed, the son, the gringo thought, not of misfortune but of a complex inheritance: the genetic General Arroyo?

Once in the midst of the battle, the old man stopped thinking, or else was thinking what no one else was thinking: of being immersed in a tide of horses, of an earthquake of snorting animals and thundering hoofs on the hard desert floor, of the stillness of the noonday clouds and the swiftness of the rebel bayonets leaving dead behind and flashing over the heavy, motionless French cannons while dazed artillerymen heard, felt, and feared the sounds rushing like a waterfall at their backs, a trembling, a deafening roar from the very mountains, an avalanche of surefooted, fearless horses, of whooping and yelling rebel troops, bullets gleaming in bandoliers on bare chests, sombreros tossed into the air like twins to the spinning sun.

The Federales were roasting in their tight French Foreign Legion uniforms, their ridiculous kepis pressing on their skulls, while the rebels on the plain, commanded by the dauntless gringo, rode straight for the artillery without so much as a glance back at the corpses littering the plain, besieged now from the air by the eternal circling buzzards of the Mexican skies and on the ground by suspicious pigs freed from the pigsty of a miserable little adobe hut and ranging free across the sterile land, bristly, phlegm-colored beasts, sniffing the air to see whether the bodies were really dead and incapable of further harm, before grunting and snuffling their way toward them to begin their feast just at the hour of the crimson sunset.

He hadn't been wounded. He wasn't dead.

This was the only thing that surprised him; his grizzled old head was filled with amazement. They rounded up the captured Federales, and the two rebel forces met in victory. This time they did not repeat the celebrations of the previous day, when the gringo had lassoed the machine gun. Maybe there were too many dead comrades on the battlefield. They were dead; not he. He wanted death and was still here, deserving of an ironic pity, helping surround what remained of the Federal regiment, feeling finally the boiling rancor he had expected: the gringo didn't die, he was the bravest among us, he marched straight on again, like yesterday, as if he wasn't afraid of anything or anybody, but he didn't die: Old Gringo!

He was not unduly surprised by what he saw and heard in the hastily erected camp beside the crumbling adobe walls of the hut from which the pigs had fled in famished terror. Arroyo told the prisoners that anyone who wanted to join the revolutionary army of Pancho Villa would be welcomed, but anyone who refused would be shot that same night, because they traveled light and didn't plan to haul around a lot of useless prisoners.

The great majority of the soldiers silently ripped off their Federal insignia and joined the Villa troops. Some resisted, and the gringo stared at them as one always stares at exceptions. Their faces were proud, or demented, or simply exhausted. They lined up behind their five officers, none of whom had budged.

Now the night wind was beginning to blow and the old gringo feared the return of his suffocating enemy. The hungry snuffling of the hogs on the battlefield filled the silence around Arroyo's proposition and the wordless actions that followed. The commanding colonel of the Federal troops walked over to Arroyo and with great dignity offered Arroyo a small, shiny, almost toy-like sword. Arroyo took it without ceremony and used it to cut a slice from the loin of one of the suckling pigs roasting over an open fire.

"You know it's a crime to execute captured officers or troops," the Colonel said.

He had sleepy, hooded green eyes and thick, blond, pointed mustaches. What a chore, the gringo thought, to keep those points waxed day and night.

"You are brave, so you have no worry," Arroyo replied, and bit into the slice of pork.

"What do your words mean?" the sleepy-eyed but haughty Colonel asked. "Bravery has nothing to do with it. I am speaking of the law."

"Of course, the law," said Arroyo, with a sad, steady gaze. "But I am asking you which is more important, the way we live or the way we die?"

The officer hesitated a moment. "Put that way, of course it is the manner in which one dies."

The old man said nothing, but he mulled over the words that might have been Arroyo's honor code and which the old man could, if he chose, take as being directed to him. Arroyo handed the sword to the gringo and invited him to eat pork as the porkers were eating the corpses on the field. The old man must have been concentrating very hard, for he was the target first of the Colonel's eye and then of his words.

"There is a brave man," the Colonel said, his eyes ready for death. Arroyo grunted and the Colonel added: "I, too, was brave. Do you admit it?" Again, Arroyo grunted. "Yet that brave old man is not going to die. I am. It could have been the other way around. But I suppose that is war."

"No," Arroyo said, finally. "That is life."

"And death," the Colonel added in a tone of presumptuous intimacy.

"As long as you don't separate them," Arroyo concluded.

The Colonel smiled and said that there was something exceptional about being too brave, whether in life or in death. He, for example, was going to die in a high, cold desert far from the sea of his native Veracruz, he who could still smell on his skin the smells of the European ships anchored in port, he was going to be executed on a night of campfires and grunting pigs. It wouldn't matter at all whether he was brave as he died; soon he would not be an annoyance to anyone. But to be too brave and still live, now that is a problem, General, that is a problem for both our armies, he said: the indecently brave man. He shows us all up. He makes all of us look a little ridiculous.

"You see," said the Federal colonel, "we all fear a

coward, and admit it; but no one admits he fears a brave man even more, because alongside him we look like cowards. It's not a bad thing to be a little afraid in battle. Then you are like everyone else. But the man who has no fear demoralizes everyone. I tell you one thing, General. Both sides should join together and, in a manner of speaking, eliminate the brave man. Honor him, yes, but not weep over him."

The words of the talkative Veracruzano did not seem to make much of an impression on Arroyo, who was squatting on his heels, rolling a pork taco in agile fingers.

"Are you that man?" he asked.

The Colonel laughed softly, if nervously. "No, of course not. Not I. Not in the least."

The old man hoped no one was looking at him eating his taco, the first food of the day since a breakfast of eggs and steaming coffee. Arroyo was recounting to them the feat of the valiant General Fierro, Villa's right arm, who had got rid of his prisoners by offering to free any man who could run from the jail across the patio to the prison wall and jump over it without getting shot by Fierro—with the condition that he couldn't shoot twice at any one man. Only three prisoners escaped. Fierro killed some three hundred men that night.

He, Arroyo, general of the Northern Division, was not going to compete with the famous General Fierro, one of Villa's favored few, the Dorados, his golden boys. He was much more modest than that. But there was riding with him a brave man, a general from the North American Civil War, the bravest man among them, everyone had seen that today. Arroyo sprang to his feet like a bobcat, speaking now not to the captured officer but to the old man. Ha! The Indiana General was always wanting to be the bravest soldier of the war, now he was going to be the bravest executioner. If he was brave facing death, he must also be brave facing life—yes?—since they were the same thing; the old man had come to Mexico to learn that, and he'd learned it, hadn't he? if he hadn't learned it by now, then his trip hadn't been worth shit, wasn't that true?

Tonight the old man would do what Fierro had done that other night. It was agreed: the officers and men of that drunken sot Huerta would be given the chance to run from the crumbling adobe wall to the creaking gate of the pigpen and from there to the field of pigs and corpses. The Indiana General would let them run as far as the gate. Then he would fire. If he missed, the Federales could flee like rabbits. If he got them, then they were dead. Brave Indiana General!

Later (not later in life, because his life was suspended, outside of time, like a drop of water on a solitary winter leaf when the only question is which will fall first: the leaf or the drop) he would say that he did the only thing he could have done. He said it to Miss Harriet in her *now*, which incorporated his impossible *then*: I did the only thing I could have done, because I hadn't had the good fortune to be killed discreetly, or naturally, or even with some nobility, by an anonymous hand on the field of battle.

"I could have been just another corpse, devoured by the hogs. God, how they grunted and shit in the cold night air."

("What was the only thing you could have done?" asked his father, mounted on the steed of the wind.

"To refuse another the death I wanted for myself.")

How he wished he were the slightly effeminate but

strangely courageous Federal colonel of the sleepy, disdainful smile and the pomaded mustaches still stiff after a day of battle, who walked to the adobe wall and stood there staring at the gringo, waiting for the command to be given.

"You see, Father, I wished to be in that man's boots."

"Run!" ordered Arroyo.

Reluctantly, the Colonel stepped away, as if all his life the crumbling and partially collapsed wall had been the final harbor to his imagination: a hearth in his own land. He walked normally at first, turning his back to Arroyo and to the old man, who held the Colt firmly in his hand. The Colonel hesitated, turned to face his enemies, and then walked backward, looking at his appointed executioner, at Arroyo, at Colonel Frutos García, at Inocencio Mansalvo, who together formed the unrecognizable face that had sentenced him without a trial. You wouldn't shoot me in the back? He was sure the old man would not dishonor himself by such an act, and both the old man and Arroyo, as he caught the gringo's eye, knew what he was thinking. Now the Colonel looked slightly ridiculous. He stumbled and fell, and then got to his feet and ran for his life.

"Shoot!" thundered Arroyo.

The old man pointed the pistol at the fleeing colonel, then at a hog. He held the sights on the hog as he pulled the trigger, and the bullet cut cleanly through the spongy, worm-infested flesh of the scavenging animal. Arroyo jumped forward with his own pistol in his hand and fired one shot at the fleeing figure of the prisoner. The remaining condemned prisoners exchanged startled glances.

The Colonel had fallen face forward. Arroyo ignored the old gringo, walked to the fallen man, and fired the

[89]

coup de grâce. The officer jerked and then was still. The captured officers and soldiers, proud or stubborn and simply exhausted, who could know? lined up against the adobe wall and the old man looked at them there, at that collection of mankind, some pissing in their pants, some with idiotic, distant expressions, one or two lighting a final cigarette, some humming a song that reminded them of wife or family. And one was smiling, not foolish, not exhausted, not brave, merely incapable of distinguishing any longer between life and death.

He was the one who caught General Arroyo's eye. "The General stared at him a long time, you remember?" Pedrito asked. "How could I forget," Mansalvo replied. "When our leader was so generous. Don't kill them, he said. Just cut off their ears as a warning, and if we ever meet them a second time, we'll know, and they won't get out of that alive."

"What a big heart our general has!"

12 As they were returning to camp, Arroyo retreated into himself like a turtle. His serape was his shell and he buried himself in it up to his nose, while he pulled his sombrero down to the painful root of his ears. All you could see were his gleaming eyes. And no one would want to look into those deep yellow wells, La Garduña said when she saw him ride into town; those weren't friendly eyes. Inocencio Mansalvo commented that victory seemed far away.

It was not a triumphal march. The only spark of hope

or happiness or sensual satisfaction or anything—if some of those things were what Arroyo really hoped to find behind his ideals of justice and behind the hasty tactics that justified but also degraded justice—lay in the forward movement of his troops, in their collective wish to leave the ruined hacienda for the next goal, to join the bulk of Villa's army, to push toward the capital, perhaps to shake the hand of their brother from the south, Zapata. Certainly Arroyo dreamed these things, or knew them because his men dreamed them. Since this morning, he had wanted to tell them to the old man, before he greeted Miss Harriet with a kiss. But he also wanted, darkly, dreamily, to prolong his stay on the hacienda where he had been born and raised.

"Will we be leaving now?" Mansalvo asked young Pedrito, as if he thought that truth was heard only from the mouths of drunks and babes.

"I don't know," the boy said. "He was born here and raised here; I guess he likes it pretty well."

"Well, the troops don't; they're getting restless," observed Colonel Frutos García.

The gringo felt the tension as soon as they started back toward the hacienda. This wasn't the time to provoke Arroyo; his sense of dramatic unity—the old writer grinned—would feel violated by another death, on top of the battle and the death of the Federal colonel. He laughed: he was no Shakespeare, not even if it was his own death. He dropped behind, with the infantry, but he also felt the tension there. Spontaneously, the tired but still malicious soldiers maneuvered the gringo toward the rear, toward the very last rows, occupied by the turncoats who had gone over to Villa but hadn't yet proved their mettle. The gringo had. For the first time, he had known fear in battle; a grave fear, not the vain fear he felt when faced with pain, or a mirror. He just smiled, and spit into the dust beyond his horse's head.

"No, I'll never forget," General Frutos García told his friends after the Revolution, after the former colonel was promoted, to make amends this way for Villa's defeat and unite the many factions of the Revolution. "The gringo had come looking for death, nothing more. What he was finding, though, was glory—and the bitter fruit of glory, envy."

Again the gringo aimed, and his dark spit raised the dust in the distance. He laughed at himself. Years ago he'd written something about the Civil War: "A simple recipe for being a good soldier: Try always to get yourself killed."

Try always to get yourself killed—that was the last thing General Frutos García said before he died in 1964 in his home in Mexico City, and his words became famous among the anecdotes told by the men who had fought in the Revolution.

The Indiana General pounded the pommel of his saddle with his fist and felt the excitement of his literary imagination sweeping over him again, a nervous tickling that rose from his boots through his long, skinny legs to the web of emotions knotted in his solar plexus. Was he here to die or to write a novel about a Mexican general and an old gringo and a Washington schoolteacher lost in the deserts of northern Mexico?

He hadn't the time or strength to imagine her now, while they were fulfilling their masculine rites of courage and death, and she had been left behind on the hacienda with the strength of an idea in her head that was in direct collision with the General's. As she loosened her tie beneath the harsh morning sun, after the bulk of the troops had left and she was alone with the drowsy garrison and the women and children, Harriet was not thinking of marching toward the next battle, or the meeting with Villa, or the triumphal march to Mexico City that constituted the thoughts and wishes of everyone else. What she had on her mind was to establish a basic schedule for the elementary instruction of the children, the salvage chores of the women, and the rebuilding chores of the men. Today—not *mañana*—the children would start learning the basic skills, the three Rs of English-language instruction: reading, writing, and 'rithmetic. The women would rummage through the huge armoires and fragrant chests the troops had dragged onto the patios before the fire and sort what was scorched from what was not, and divide everything neatly, putting the unscorched articles back where they belonged and cutting down and sewing the damaged clothing for their personal use. The men would whitewash the walls as soon as repairs were completed, and clean away the stains and remove the ashes. And she, Miss Harriet Winslow, would set the example; she would be the symbol around which all the work of restoring the hacienda would revolve.

In her haste, Señora Miranda had left behind a small coffer hidden in the hollow of the wall behind her bed, protected by a huge crucifix that had burned, saving the coffer but revealing what it hid. The jewel box contained several beautiful pearl necklaces. Harriet was repelled by the idea of jewels hidden behind the figure of the dying Christ (who, furthermore, safeguarded the carnal passions of the wealthy couple sleeping at His feet); an unholy congress between God's suffering and worldly possessions. So she placed the coffer in full view, not in the glittering ballroom, where it seemed to her she would be coupling luxury with luxury (to her manner of thinking, if not idolatry, at least bad taste), but in the simple vaulted passageway leading to the ballroom. She displayed the coffer on a small walnut table in this corridor, in solitary, but tempting, splendor. That it was tempting, Miss Winslow admitted, but temptation was necessary to teach these people that private property should be respected and that learning this is as important as learning to read.

The work of the morning sped by, and then came the hour of a lunch that was too large and exotic for Miss Harriet's taste (bubbling casseroles, chili sauces, fragrant herbs, and warm, steaming tortillas), and before they asked for permission to go to the fields to tend their poor crops and look after their own houses, she played her strongest, her most surprising, her most definitive card. She called them into the ballroom and told them they would meet here regularly—once a week, if matters so required—and they would elect their own officials, a secretary and a treasurer; they would form committees to be in charge of cattle raising, education, maintenance, and also supplies. They must get started at once. When the legitimate owners returned, they would find an accomplished fact, the hacienda would have an organization that spoke for the people who lived and worked there, and would protect their rights. That would come later. But today, when he returned, General Arroyo would find that the people were already governing themselves, truly governing themselves, not talking a lot of vague ideas about how things would be when the war was over and then came the millennium, no, right now!

listen to me, he will go on fighting until he dies, he will never stop fighting, even if he wins, but you will still be here. He says that he liberated you. Well, now you show him he's right, even if it means challenging what he says.

After Miss Harriet spoke, they stared at her from behind campesino masks that didn't say yes and didn't say no or we understand or we don't understand or we have our own ways or we can learn without you. No, they said none of these things, as she announced that class was dismissed and they would see each other tomorrow.

Rapidly, she buttoned the neck of her blouse, but the people did not leave immediately, they stood talking quietly among themselves, sorry for her but not really wanting to show it, as La Garduña said, who could only watch these goings-on with amazement, everyone wondering whether they ought to tell her today why tomorrow it would be impossible to do what she had said today.

Poor señorita, one woman said; she is nice, but she does not know what day tomorrow is.

They felt sorry for her, and laughed like playful little birds.

Now she sits and remembers.

She yielded to the siesta; she felt degraded, immoral, for falling asleep at four in the afternoon: her mind was still in the ballroom, she alone, and seeking in vain the eyes that would share the uneasiness of her dreams, when she wanted to get up but felt as if a hand were holding her back, keeping her captive in the bed, soaking the sheet that covered her damp, naked, musky body smelling of dead magnolia petals and dank cellars, her body, dragging her back into sleep.

Harriet Winslow always awakened with a certain feeling of guilt for what she had said or left unsaid the previous day: guilt for the errors and omissions of the day gone by.

Today, conflict and sensation were worse than ever, and the question that held her—against her will (she was convinced of that), lying in bed at four o'clock in the afternoon—was one that she had formulated before: When was I most happy?

She did not often ask herself the question, because she always remembered her mother's beatific *ritornello*: Happiness prevails. In spite of that, she answered herself: "I was happiest when my adored father left us and I could be the responsible one; I felt that now everything depended on me; it was I who had to sacrifice, to strive, to temporize, and not only on my own behalf, but on behalf of all those who love me and whom I love in return." Happy fulfilling my duty. This link between her dream and her actions brought her closer to the image she wanted to preserve of her father. It brought her closer to everything he had said, at random, at the family table: that kind of rambling philosophy everyone hears and learns at home: life is difficult, life is easy, everything will turn out well, order will triumph, charity begins at home, do unto others as . . . ; strong, thrifty, wise: God-fearing, sober Methodists, no baroque altars here, God-fearing; these things became her duty when her father left, more than her mother's, whom Harriet could not bear as a dejected shadow but whom she loved once again when she reflected the light of innocence, the quasi-simple happiness of her daughter's youth, before the father marched away and was declared missing in action.

"Why do you stay on here with me, Harriet? Aren't you bored?"

In Mexico, her duty was more than ever her duty. But something was lacking in her dream. There was something more, something without which simple duty was not enough. She tried to invoke a different dream within her dream, a light, a back yard strewn with fallen dogwood blossoms, a moan from a black pit.

The old man, on the road back, was not thinking of her. Nor Arroyo. Suddenly, she awakened. Before she saw the faces or heard the voices, she murmured, still in her dream, that unless you attempt to organize life as soon as you awaken, you'll have to confront your dreams. My baby's afraid, oh, she's so afraid!: La Garduña, brutal, rouged face, small sharp teeth, was weeping beside her; she was shaking her, she was telling her a hysterical, melodramatic tale she couldn't understand; she understood only one thing: Help us, miss, my baby is dying.

A small bluish bundle, skin tinged with pain, the dying child, choking to death while the alkaline wind of the desert blew outside, and Harriet, on her knees in the railroad car, as in a dream, imagined herself a child, the daughter of a military man in the field, ill, in a railroad car that served as house and kitchen and now as hospital: the child-that-was-she was choking and everyone was talking at once, a grief-stricken Garduña, the woman with the moon face: Save her, miss, we don't know what else to do, it came on all at once, La Garduña's baby girl, she's only two years old, don't let her die, she's choking, she caught a draft, look at her color; and Harriet, helpless, no medicine, no syringe, nothing except a small packet of aspirin in her valise, toothpaste, brushes for her hair and her clothing and her teeth: La Garduña's knife-sharp teeth and Harriet's fresh, clean mouth; no medicine, she could only save the child with her body, run get the aspirin, but we gave her aspirin, and scrubbing and cleansing with twigs, and there is no priest here, he ran away. My body, Harriet thought: when shall I bathe my body, when will I be able to wash, I'm covered with filth and death, death and dream, dreaming of my father missing in the Cuban campaign, and his empty grave in Arlington, carrying dream and filth and death and fear ever since I disembarked in Veracruz, Cuba and Veracruz, always the back yards of my country, occupied by my country because our destiny is to be strong with the weak, the port of Veracruz occupied by the United States Marines following a supposed insult to the Stars and Stripes.

"Did you have any difficulty when you disembarked, Miss Winslow?"

"Did the occupation authorities poke and pry, Miss Winslow?"

"Did they ask you, rather rudely, where you were going and what was the motive for your trip, Miss Winslow?"

"Did you show them with pride the notarized papers that prove you are able to fend for yourself and earn your own living, Miss Winslow?"

"Did you tell them they needn't worry about repatriating a lost and hungry American girl; this girl had come to teach the English tongue to the children of a wealthy family, Miss Winslow?"

"Did you tell them you weren't a nurse but a schoolteacher, what you had always been, an instructress, not a governess, Miss Winslow?"

"Did you see the shell-pocked walls of the old prison of San Juan de Ulúa, thinking that you might end up there yourself, Miss Winslow?"

"Did you realize that the walls of the city are also pockmarked by recent cannon fire from gringo warships, Miss Winslow?"

"Did you realize that the white candles with white rosettes and flowers in the streets marked the places where the cadets of the Naval College of Veracruz fell, Miss Winslow?"

"Did two Marines escort you in a carriage to the train station through streets filled with dog packs and gathering buzzards, Miss Winslow?"

"Did a Mexican sharpshooter fire at you from a flat roof, and before one of the Marines fell dead beside you, staining your rose-colored blouse with the blood of the wheat fields of Ohio, did he manage to tell you where he was from, Miss Winslow?"

"Trembling, did you board the train that would carry you to Mexico City, Miss Winslow, amid priests and young men and businessmen who were fleeing from but fell captive to confused stories of an alien revolution, Miss Winslow?"

"Did you see how they took the young men who wanted to go to Veracruz and instead sent them by train to Chihuahua, Miss Winslow?"

"Did they tell you they wanted to fight the Yankees in Veracruz but instead were impressed by Huerta to fight against Villa in the north, Miss Winslow?"

"Did you understand anything that was happening in your back yard, Miss Winslow?"

A carpet of dogwood blossoms. A deep, black moan. She could give only her mind to these things, because she had to press her mouth to the sick child's mouth, suck, kiss, air, in and out, receive, spit out, the obstruction, the child's phlegm, tell herself, it doesn't matter, I have been vaccinated, the baby hasn't, spit out the phlegm, viscous, black, blue as the tiny body of the child, think of her arrival in Mexico, not about what she was doing, and the child cried, strong and clear, as if she were newborn.

La Garduña kissed Miss Harriet's hands. "God bless you, señorita!"

"It's a miracle," said the woman with the moon face.

"No, no," Harriet protested. "It was something that had to be done. It wasn't a miracle, but it must have been predestined. It may be what I came to Mexico to do. Now give her salt water, and sugar water. The little girl will live."

The little girl will live because I held her by the feet and spanked her buttocks, hard! The child will live because my spanking jarred the phlegm from her throat. The child was crying and begging me not to spank her, don't spank me anymore. But I enjoyed spanking her. My anger saved her. I never had children. But I saved the child. It's difficult for me to find love in what I don't know. I conceive and protect love like a great mystery.

This is what Harriet Winslow told General Tomás Arroyo one night.

"I will never have children."

13 The women covered their faces as the weary columns returned at dawn, dragging themselves back to camp.

Pedrito remembered that the women watching them return were laughing silently, and only the youngest girls revealed their round faces, red as apples in the cold desert dawn.

"They're in love," Colonel García told the young boy who didn't understand very clearly what love was: they were counting their men to see how many had returned, who had been lost.

"My poor father, lost in Cuba."

"My poor son, dead in Veracruz."

There were new men, unsure of their ground, the prisoners who had come over to Villa's side, content simply to reach a village and make new friends. A revived La Garduña, arranging the bunch of dead roses at her breast, was there to welcome them, to say that life is for the living, that all of them were like her, they had never left their villages before but now they were traveling everywhere, conceiving a child in Durango, giving birth in Juárez, losing it in Chihuahua: from the beginning of time, they had been isolated in their forgotten villages, their huts in the desert, their hovels in the mountains, and now everybody knew everybody, they were riding around in trains to boot: Long live the Revolution, and General Tomás Arroyo!

The old gringo saw all the welcoming faces and felt a sharp stab of recognition, stronger than he had felt in the ballroom. One song was heard again and again around the campfires: *Along came the whirlwind and swept us all away.*

"I don't know whether the gringo and Señorita Harriet

realized that the Revolution was a wind that tore men and women from their roots and whirled them far from their settled dust and their old cemeteries and their quiet villages," Colonel García said to his friend Inocencio Mansalvo the day the brave guerrilla from Torreón, Coahuila, was hanged.

"They must have known," Inocencio replied. "They had to remember that Americans always moved West, but until the Revolution, Mexicans had never moved at all."

Mansalvo was caught robbing gold from a derailed train in Charco Blanco; he was hanged on the spot, his leather pouch stuffed with stolen coins. "Don't lay a hand on it," said Colonel Frutos García, who gave the order. "He was a brave man. He deserves to take his money with him."

"I'm sorry, Inocencio. You won't be moving anymore."

In his own lifetime, the old gringo was going to tell Miss Winslow, he had seen an entire nation move from New York to Ohio to the battlegrounds of Georgia and the Carolinas and then to California, where the continent, sometimes even destiny, ended.

Mexicans had never moved, except as criminals or slaves. Now they were moving, to fight and make love. La Garduña raised both arms high to capture the attention of a former Federal soldier with full mustaches who had struck her fancy.

The old gringo found Miss Harriet seated before the mirror in the sleeping car, pinning up her auburn hair. He was stopped by the image, fascinated by the nearness of fragrant, powdered, soft, woman's flesh, and musical laughter.

"Don't look at me that way. The women brought jugs and jugs of water and gave me a bath. I haven't bathed since I arrived here. And you know that next to godliness, the greatest virtue is . . ."

"Of course," the old man murmured. Their eyes met in the mirror. "I thought a lot about you last night. You were very real in my thoughts. I think I even dreamed about you. I felt as close to you as a . . ."

"As a father?" Now it was her turn to interrupt. "As close as that?" she asked, with no hint of emotion. But immediately she lowered her eyes. "I'm glad you're back."

They heard several sharp reports in succession—impossible to know how many, as explosions detonate time and shatter seconds—and Miss Harriet clutched her hairpins as a shipwrecked sailor clings to a lifeboat. Nothing seemed more ridiculous than to drop things: the pins. Her unpinned hair fell to her shoulders, and she gripped the gringo's hand. "Oh, God, they've come back!"

"Who?"

"The other soldiers. Oh, this is what I feared. They won't be able to tell who is on what side."

"They will take you, Miss Harriet, for an American adventuress who came to Mexico in search of cheap thrills."

Such a ridiculous idea dissipated Harriet Winslow's fear; she pressed the old man's hand. She thought of death, intermittently. He gazed deep into her gray eyes.

"I swear to you I accepted this position before anything had happened, before my beau Mr. Delaney was found guilty of federal fraud or his story came out, I swear it . . ."

"I don't want to know anything about that," the old man said, and pressed his lips to Harriet's cheek.

"But you mentioned Leland Stanford. You know these things happen all the time. But I swear I had already made my decision. I came here freely, I want you to know that . . ."

Over the old man's shoulder, still in his arms, she saw Arroyo standing at the entrance to the compartment, partially hidden by the heavy blue silk drapes lining this regal carriage. Then she heard a faint rustle behind Arroyo and a slim, soft feminine hand took him by the arm. Miss Harriet shut her own lips tight and caught a glimpse of the blue rebozo of the woman with the moon face.

The explosions continued, increasing in volume and frequency: she freed herself from the old man's tender embrace and finished buttoning her blouse. She wondered what was happening but wanted to hide her fear.

"Maybe it *is* the Federales," said the old man, who had no fear of making his fear public. "Then may the devil have pity on us all."

"No." The tiny woman with the moon face and slim, soft hands had come in from the General's compartment. "It is only fireworks."

It was the day of the village's patron saint, she said, a great feast day throughout the region, they would see, and she led them from the stationary car into the air thick with gunpowder exploded by the same men who the day before were firing Winchesters smuggled from Texas. The acrid air held both gunpowder and incense, and a group of masked children surrounded Miss Harriet, hobbling around in imitation of the dance of the little old men. The old gringo turned and looked toward the railroad car.

Arroyo stood on the platform, a long black cigar clamped between his teeth, bare-chested, haloed by smoke, looking at the old man, looking at Harriet Winslow, looking at the two of them. The Indians of the north danced monotonously before the chapel, rattles jingling at their ankles, as the old man followed Harriet to the ruined shell of the hacienda, along the devastated colonnade where the village women, with a mixture of embarrassment and pleasure, were trying on the old dresses she had authorized them to mend: the fiesta always offered an excuse for anything, even Harriet wanted to show the gringo what she had accomplished, to conquer the dream, conquer the past, organize the future—save a life, but she didn't want to tell him that, let him find out for himself.

The pearls were not there; she was shamed, enraged, her hand searching the empty coffer. Everything she had dreamed, planned, won, evaporated in bitterness (now she sits alone and remembers).

"The spoils," she said. "That's all they want."

"Don't be afraid," the old man said suddenly.

"She has nothing to fear." Arroyo, wearing nothing but chamois trousers and high boots, was buckling heavy holsters on each side of his flat, naked belly.

"You will forgive me that I did not dress; I was in a hurry. I was afraid you would do something you would regret, señorita."

"You have your booty," she replied, proud (she remembers), haughty (now she sits alone), and happy that he had overheard her. "It *is* the only thing they want, isn't it? All the rest is nothing but talk."

Arroyo looked at the empty coffer. He looked at the

old man. Roughly, he seized Harriet's wrist. Harriet, too, looked at the old man, seeking his help, but he knew his moment with this woman had come and gone; she might still have time to nestle in his arms and to love him as a wife or a daughter, it didn't matter; it was too late; he saw Arroyo's face, Arroyo's body, Arroyo's hand, and he surrendered. His son and his daughter.

"You, a horseman: would you take a woman who's been hurt, or one you pity?"

Arroyo still gripped Harriet's wrist; she would struggle against him if the old man did not heed Arroyo's first words and protect her; but the specter of appearing ridiculous intruded. She let him know that she was strong, too, that he was leading her against her will, not kicking and protesting but strong like him, strong in any situation he could create now. He led Harriet and the old gringo from the house into the burning day, hazy, dusty, and dark, through the men and women making their way on bloody knees toward the chapel already thronged with people. Now she sits alone and remembers that more than the return of the Federales she feared this fatally foreign land whose only reality was the stubborn determination never to be anything other than its eternal, miserable, chaotic self: she smelled it, she sensed it. This was Mexico.

The old man could smell Harriet's fear and he imagined what his own father, the thundering Calvinist, would have said when he entered this chapel:

"Oh, the extravagance, the horror of the prodigality, the idolatrous waste of the fruits of Our Lord in this baroque excess, gold leaf in every nook and cranny of the altar, the ornamented walls, gilded bas-reliefs of figs and apples and cherubim and trumpets, this diarrhea of

Mexican and Spanish gold in the middle of a desert of dust and pigs and thorns and bare feet and ragged shawls and burnt sacrifices!"

The dead Christ reposed in his cage of glass. The King of Kings, naked, partially covered by His cape of red velvet. He had bled after His death. His sacrifice had not negated the bondage of His life, of His incarnation, of His terrible plea for well-being while suffering the preordained damnation of the hapless, earthly body that should have been thinking of the Father: the father in the sky, horseman of the sky, mounted forever on a Calvinist pulpit, his wooden horse, his Clavileño of judgments and predestination. The American señorita saved La Garduña's sick baby: a miracle; a necessity. The old gringo saw a cold, undeclared complicity in Miss Harriet's eyes as they were reunited in their altarless religions of the North, where Jesus the Redeemer lived forever liberated from the flesh, from image, from painting, an ineffable spirit borne on the altars of music: a true God who, unlike the Mexican Christ, could never bleed, eat, fornicate, or evacuate.

Arroyo pulled Harriet close to him and pointed to the flickering, self-devouring, excremental altar where the Virgin neither bled nor fornicated, the purest Mother of God, in all her glazed porcelain glory, draped in robes of gold and blue and crowned with pearls; now she sits alone and remembers those pearls that she had rescued only yesterday, rescued from the blackened bedchamber of the absent mistress of the house and offered in an open coffer as a temptation and as a monument to thrift and honor.

"Who paid for all this . . . this . . . this extravagance?" was all she could say to hide her shame, her accusation of theft, her having shown herself to be the true great-niece of old Halston. They save the whole year, señorita, they go hungry to have their fiesta on the appointed day. Arroyo was raised here, the son of silence and misfortune.

A never-ending fiesta, a proliferating energy that fed on its own excesses of color and fever and sacrifice. The old gringo did not want to read omens or perceive destinies in the thronging life surrounding him, pressing and pushing him slowly into the chapel, a strong and irradicable snaking of faith incarnate and sacrifice and waste, toward the altar, farther and farther from them, the old man separated from Arroyo and Harriet, the man and woman together now, embraced by a blind destiny the old gringo could understand in Harriet's face but not on his. Arroyo's face. The old gringo's face, saying to Arroyo: Take her, take my daughter. Into the middle of the kneeling penitents, the thick incense and scapulars, rolled a perfect silver peso, and young Pedrito, on all fours like a little animal, scrambled after it, fearful of losing his only treasure.

14 The peso went rolling toward the edge of the small plaza. Pedrito heard a distant pianola; even in the confusion of the fiesta, he knew where the music was coming from. He hummed along. Who didn't know that tune? *Sobre las olas*, Tomás Arroyo whispered into Harriet Winslow's ear. *The loveliest night of the year*, Harriet Winslow whispered into his, as the pianola tinkled away in some abandoned and invisible corner of the hacienda;

a man and a woman in the ballroom the General had saved from the fire and presented, she said, to the night, to the moonlit night.

They danced slowly, repeated in mirrors like a sphere of blades that cuts wherever it is grasped.

"Look. It's me."

"Look. It's you."

"Look. It's us."

They danced, embraced, in the waning hours of the fiesta. She was dancing the slow waltz with him but also with her father: *I am dancing with my father, just back from Cuba,* decorated in Cuba, promoted in Cuba, saved by Cuba, savior of Cuba.

"We went to save Cuba."

"We've come to save Mexico."

Harriet dancing this night with her ramrod-straight, decorated, brave father at a soirée welcoming the heroes of Cuba, tricolor rosettes on the bosoms of all the women, WELCOME HOME HEROES OF SAN JUAN HILL, her uniformed father, with stiff mustaches and hair smelling of cologne, proud of his slender daughter in her whirl of taffeta, Captain Winslow with a slightly different scent, and she, burying her nose in her father's neck, smelling the city of Washington there, that false Acropolis of marble and domes and columns sunk in the wet mud of a pernicious tropics that dared not say its name: a Southern suffocation, a jungle of marble like a grandiose and empty cemetery, the temples of justice and the government sinking into an equatorial, devouring, spreading tangle of undergrowth: a vegetal cancer rooted in the foundations of Washington, a city moist as the crotch of an aroused Negress: Harriet buried her nose in Tomás Arroyo's neck and smelled a Negress's swollen, velvety

[109]

sex: Captain Winslow, I am very lonely, you may have me at your pleasure.

As they danced, Tomás Arroyo squeezed the foreign woman's waist and pressed closer to the warmth of her belly. He imagined the tangled growth there as a beautiful forest he would always see from afar, and from behind a door of mirrors the boy Tomás Arroyo came out to dance with his mother, his mother, his father's legitimate wife, his mother, the straight and clean woman without a weight of clouds on her shoulders, without a crown of cold winds on her brow, without eyes ashen from the sun, but clean, no more than that, a clean woman, dressed cleanly, combed cleanly, shod cleanly, dancing with her son the waltz *Sobre las olas* that they had heard so often far away in the big house, where they could keep out prying eyes but could not keep in the sounds of the music.

The music was so intense that it gave voice to the almost always silent earth and allowed them—look, it's us—to give themselves to love without fear of being heard. Tomás Arroyo put his tongue in Harriet Winslow's ear.

Then she felt the fear of knowing beauty and danger at the same time.

Fear became pleasure only by having been thought. Her true fear was that nothing more would happen. Tomás Arroyo put his tongue in her ear, and Harriet Winslow felt a terrible sense of absence, not that of her father, but that of the old gringo.

"I shall conquer General Tomás Arroyo before I go back to the routine of life at home." But the old man had told her that in Mexico there was nothing to subdue and nothing to save.

"That's what's difficult for us to understand, because our ancestors conquered nothing, while here there was a civilized race. That's what my father told me following the War of 1848. 'Mexico is not a bad country. It's just a different country.' "

A different tongue, in her ear: heard, felt, moist, sinuous, a tongue Harriet accepted but from which she also fled, concentrating on her own feeling for the changing seasons. She was dancing in Arroyo's arms, but at this very instant she could transmit a sense of seasons that didn't exist here: in the summers of her youth she had danced near the cool murmurs in Rock Creek Park; on a sled she swooped down the snowy slopes of Meridian Hill Park; hand in hand with her mother she walked along Fourteenth Street, shopping in little aromatic Greek shops for the nuts and apples of autumn; on a spring day that carried flying pollen and the marvel of cherry trees she visited Arlington Cemetery and looked at an empty grave.

She pressed closer to Tomás Arroyo, as if she were afraid of losing something, but she held her head away to see her own wild surprise in the eyes of the Mexican.

"I've been here before but I won't know it until I leave."

He whispered in her ear, did she like to dream?

Yes, she said; in her dreams she was ageless.

Something even better: when she wakened, she didn't know where she was.

Arroyo remembered only one season: it was always the same, time here didn't have those signposts and that explained the violent need to mark time with unforgettable wounds, wounds that hurt even after they had healed: it was his life.

"Forgive me, little gringa. I don't know many things of the world. Sometimes I am very moody. I understand and I feel some things very deeply, little gringa, very deeply, because if I don't feel them, I don't have any way to understand."

They danced the dance as if they were dancing a story. She said things into his ear in English, as if he could understand them merely because she spoke as if they had all happened before: *I shall never see Delaney again. When I talk about going home, I don't mean I will do the same things again. I shall take home your time, Arroyo, and the old man's time; I shall guard them, Arroyo. You don't know it, but I shall be mistress of all the times I won here. As I understand it better, I shall grow more beautiful and happier; as I stroll with your times, safeguarding them, along the banks of Rock Creek in the summer and along the snowy paths of Meridian Hill in the winter and stopping on Sixteenth Street in the fall and spring before an abandoned house where the setting sun plays with the changing reflections of movement on the windowpanes. You will forgive me then for having kept your time, Arroyo, or you will degrade everything by asking me to give myself to you in exchange for a man's life . . .*

He didn't ask; neither did he agree. This would not be only a man's story from now on. A presence (my presence, said Harriet) will alter the story. *I only hope that I also give him a secret and a danger that events in themselves could never guarantee.*

"Loneliness is an absence of time."

Arroyo held her close and wished he could tell her everything he was thinking, so that when she left she would have no complaints but would feel she was mistress of everything she had won here. He would ask her to keep his time, his, Tomás Arroyo's, when he could no longer do it. And the old man's time. His, too—Arroyo nodded. She would accept. They would exchange times, smiled the Mexican: the one who lived would guard the time of the other two, that would be all right, wouldn't it? the General asked, almost timidly, almost tenderly, wouldn't it, whatever happened?

When the two gringos left Mexico, he wanted them to say: "I have been here. This land will always be a part of me now." That's what I ask of them. I swear: it's the only thing I ask. Don't forget us. But, more than anything, be us and still be yourself . . . and fuck it all.

Then he said what she feared he would say. "It's up to you whether or not the gringo returns to his country alive."

She didn't hear what Arroyo added (He's stubborn. He's a brave man. And he's a bad example to my men) but what he did not add (*I won't spend this night without you. I want you, more than you can imagine, little gringa. I'll tell you how much. I want you like I want my mother back alive again. That much. Forgive me, but I will do whatever I have to do to have you tonight, my beautiful gringa*), because Arroyo didn't realize that Harriet was dancing with a decorated, dignified officer fresh from his bath, and Arroyo, on the contrary, had abandoned his decent and respectable mother: Harriet saw Arroyo pushing out from between the legs of all women burdened by cares and shadows.

When she moved from Arroyo's arms, she saw herself in a ballroom lined with mirrors. She saw herself entering the mirrors without looking at herself, because in reality she was entering a dream and in that dream her father was still alive and there was an empty grave in Arlington.

She looked at Arroyo and kissed him with wild surprise. The boy dropped the silver peso but the coin didn't ring against the cobbles because a freckled, bony hand covered with white hairs caught it in the air.

15

He felt humiliated in the patient presence of the moon-faced woman in the blue rebozo. Her moist eyes revealed a deep, wise self-possession. A soldier's woman; he had known them in his life and read about them in the epics of the past. But now she touched him with her slim, soft hand, asking without words that he pretend nothing was happening, that they just be there, in the glittering glass cage of the ballroom, caged like the Christ in His transparent coffin, or like the departed landowners who every year held a grand ball for the ladies and gentlemen of Chihuahua and El Paso, and even Mexico City.

Pretending. He felt degraded, but not she.

"Sometimes he feels lonely; always he is a man," said the woman with the moon face.

"Don't you satisfy him?" asked the old gringo, cruelly.

She was not offended. "Men and women are different."

"That isn't true, and you know it. I don't espouse the cause of feminism. One of the reasons I am here, señora, is that I fear a world filled with maddened suffragettes: an intolerable matriarchy. But the fact is, we both try to get the best of each other. It's just that you do it more secretively than we do. That's all."

The woman with the moon face acquiesced. She was satisfied, but Arroyo wasn't: not because he didn't love her, but because he had asked her to show she loved him by accepting that he needed love more than she.

"You are not a country woman."

He took the woman's hands and examined them.

"No. I know how to read and write."

"Where did he find you?"

"He didn't find me. I found him. He rode into my village like a young stallion, dark and silky. Then the village was taken by the Federal troops. I saved him from a horrible death, believe me, Indiana General."

"Gratitude."

"Then I am the one who is grateful. I never imagined any man could love me like that. It is not the custom in my village. It was a sad place where even married couples went to bed in secret, in silence, in darkness.

She told him that, in contrast, Arroyo was naked, even when he had clothes on. As he was a silent man, even when he spoke.

"I had to save him so he could save me. We are together and I understand him."

"I am glad."

They stood without speaking. The old gringo tried to imagine what Arroyo would be saying to Harriet while this woman was talking to him, not imagining that Arroyo might also be wondering what the woman was telling the old gringo while Arroyo was telling Harriet how the woman with the moon face had saved him when he was hiding from the Federales during the first days of the campaign against Huerta in the north.

They had surrounded the village and Arroyo knew they would kill him if they found him. He was the only rebel left in the village, and he took refuge in a cellar. He heard them walking over his head and heard them kill his captured comrades. He heard everything, because the cellar echoed like a seashell. Then they boarded everything shut.

Arroyo did not understand what was happening. Had they sentenced this village to death because it had served as a barracks for the revolutionaries? They had shut him up in this cellar, not knowing he was there. He had always had a good sense of smell. He smelled the dogs sleeping in a corner; they had been awakened by the hammering. They were big and ugly and gray, with jaws like steel traps. He had never seen anything take so long to come awake; it was as if they had lain forgotten in the cellar since the beginning of time.

He thought they must have been left there for him, that they were his spirit *nahuals*, animals that could take any shape. In truth, they were two ugly, ferocious gray mastiffs that their owner had put in the cellar because the Federales stole everything he owned, and this man loved his dogs more than his silver—had he had any— or his wife—which he had.

"Don't look at me like that, gringa."

"That's how I feel."

"You are here of your own will."

"Yes, but only for the reason I gave you. You know that."

"Ah, yes, because you like the old man."

"I do. He feels such pain. At least I understand that."

"And mine?"

"You inflict pain. But I will help him however I can. That's why I'm here."

"Are you going to save him as she saved me?"

"I don't know how she saved you."

Arroyo and the dogs watched each other. The dogs knew he was there. He knew the dogs were there. Dogs always attack or bark. Amazingly, they didn't bark, they didn't attack, they merely watched Arroyo as if they feared him as much as he feared them. Maybe they thought he was another animal, or maybe their owner had taught them to fear anyone who smelled like a soldier. Who knows? Dogs have more than five senses. Arroyo said he wouldn't be telling her this story if it weren't so strange.

Arroyo had thought the day would never end. He hadn't moved; he had communicated to the dogs that he was as strong as they, and that for now he wouldn't do them any harm. Night came and he realized the dogs had been waiting because they could sense him better than he could see them. They growled. They sensed that Arroyo was getting ready for them. They barked savagely, and leapt toward him. Arroyo fired. His bullets caught them in the air, like two heavy eagles. He emptied his pistol. They fell, growling viciously. He looked at them. He was afraid that someone had heard the shots and would kill him as he had killed them. He nudged them and rolled them over with the toe of his boot. Two ferocious, monstrous dogs.

"I tell you this because I hope that at last you will understand me."

"You know why I'm here."

Days passed and Arroyo could hear military orders

issued above his head, especially orders for the firing squad. Meanwhile, he was dying of hunger, with an empty pistol in one hand and two dead dogs at his feet. He wished he had one bullet left. It would be better than eating his dead enemies.

"Now I will believe anything you tell me."

"You are not my prisoner."

"I know that now."

"Believe what I tell you. You can leave whenever you want."

That night, he heard someone rapping on the nailed boards. A woman's voice told him not to despair. She would set him free as soon as the danger had passed. Do not give up hope. What she didn't know was that Arroyo could have eaten the dogs. But he listened to her voice and told himself he had to believe in her, he must not insult her by doubting her, and besides, she was his only hope. He must not eat that carrion; he could not tell her later: I believed in you but I didn't believe you were going to save me, and now I kiss your lips with the same lips that ate a dog's flesh.

"Understand me, and forgive this passing love I feel for you, gringa."

"I know. I, too, know how to save a man. Though the consequences are different. You know very well what you must tell me, General."

He told her that there had been two possible deaths the night following the battle. One was the gringo's. The other, the colonel of the Federal troops. Either of the two could have died.

"I came back to tell you that the Colonel died like a brave man."

"Your dream of honor never ends."

(Now she is alone and remembers: That's not life as I understand it. So did she now, finally, understand life, after being loved by him?)

"You are vain, and sometimes foolish, but you are also sincere and vulnerable. I know that, now I have loved you. I understand that, but not the way you understand life. You celebrate death over life."

"I am alive. Because of a woman yesterday, and because of you today."

No. She shook her auburn hair. He was alive today because the perfect moment for his death had not yet come. He must not let it pass. The most important thing in Arroyo's life would be, not how he lived, but how he died.

"You are right. I hope you will see me die, my gringa."

"I told you. I would rather see you dead than the old man."

"He is very old."

"But I don't know how to judge his pain. Yours, I do."

"You have been judging me ever since you came here."

"I shall not do it anymore, I swear. That is my promise in exchange for yours, General Arroyo."

"You talk too much, my pretty gringa. As a boy, I knew only silence. You have more words than feelings, I think."

"That isn't true. I love children. I am good with them."

"Then let's have one."

They both laughed, and he kissed her again, entombed in her mouth as in a cellar of menacing dogs, devouring her tongue with the same hunger he had felt then.

"Don't you like it, gringuita? With or without promises, don't you like it? Tell me, my precious gringuita, my loving, sorrowing gringuita, making real love for the first time, don't tell me no, my glorious beauty, doesn't your love like my love?"

"Yes!"

Arroyo cried out in ecstasy, and the woman with the moon face pressed the old man's hand and said of Arroyo what everyone said about the gringo: "He came here to die."

"Captain Winslow, I am very lonely and you may have me at your pleasure."

As the old gringo was walking back to the railroad car, he saw Arroyo, alone, laughing, swaggering around the dusty camp, unaware of what his enemy might be doing or saying. But the gringo imagined, feared, that the General was strutting like a cock to let him know the American woman was his, he had got the best of the fucking gringos, now he, Arroyo, the macho, had fucked the American woman and with one quick ejaculation washed away the defeats of Chapultepec and Buenavista.

But Harriet did not share the old man's thoughts. When Arroyo left her, the woman with the moon face had returned to the compartment where the two women slept; Harriet was shocked and ashamed. This was his real woman.

"You must understand." The slim, soft hands that were so essential a part of her nature forbade protest. "They were whipped with the flat blade of a machete if they were heard making love. Sometimes they almost killed them. They had to make love and have their pleasure in silence. I tell you this as a woman. They were less than animals. I was the first woman he ever loved without being afraid of his words and his sighs. He will never forget how he cried out with pleasure the first time he came in me and no one beat him for it. I will not forget it either, Señorita Harriet. I will never interfere with his love, because it would be to interfere with my own love. But until tonight, with you, he had never cried out again. That did make me afraid, I must confess it now, before it is too late and my premonition turns into something else. Tomás Arroyo is the son of silence. His real words are the papers that he understands better than anyone, even though he can't read them. I always feared that he would come back here, to the place where he was born. Who knows what can happen when someone returns to the home he has left for good?"

As she did not know how to answer, Harriet made a weak attempt to tell the woman that she, too, had had a lover in her country, an honest, tender man, a distinguished and responsible man, a . . . She looked into the eyes of the woman with the moon face, and could not continue.

"You are free, gringa," Arroyo had said as he left her that evening, and she had answered no, that was not really love; but what would she tell him if he came back again tonight, a little drunk, to tell her that once was not enough, that the old man's pain was nothing compared to his pain, the pain of not having her again, of wanting her again, of imagining her naked in his arms, caressing her . . .

"Now you have nothing left to desire or imagine, General Arroyo."

"Don't punish me, come on, please."

"Would you rather imagine me? Now you sound like a man I once knew. He, too, preferred to imagine me, to have other women so I would remain his ideal woman. Maybe it's my fate to live in men's imaginations."

Arroyo said he didn't know anything about Harriet's past, nor did he want to. Maybe she felt she was getting even, too. We are all resentful, some more than others, Tomás Arroyo told her. We all want revenge. Here we call it by its name. What do you call it?"

"Charity . . . fate . . ." murmured Harriet Winslow.

He admitted that yes, he had wanted to kill the old gringo the night of the battle, to be able to tell her he died like a coward. What did she really want? To have a father like the old gringo, or to be like her father with Arroyo? She trembled when she heard this and said to him: Speak, speak, say something else, anything, but not what you just said.

Arroyo thought before he decided to love her that he would never know why the old gringo had refused to kill the Colonel, why he had lost the chance to win the General's confidence.

"That was the first thing I said to myself, gringa." Immediately, he had had second thoughts. "The second was: Arroyo, if you kill the old gringo, you will never have the pretty American. Then a little devil got into my head and told me, Arroyo, maybe the two things are the same. Neither of you wants to lose that woman. And you both know she will never make love with a murderer."

This angered her. How did Arroyo count his dead? Did the dead of a new day eradicate the bodies of the previous day? Each morning, was it a blur of blood and a new death count? Tomorrow and tomorrow . . . He said that nothing he had told her mattered. He could have said anything he wanted. He could have invented another fate for the old man. She cried that he was attacking her deepest faith. She begged him to believe her; she didn't think the way he did; it was too difficult to go on; they mustn't be together again; once, to make each other a promise and give each other pleasure, she accepted that, but not to reinvent a destiny, his—worse, that of another. That was not according to her faith, sobbed Harriet Winslow. Only God can do that:

"Not a man like you."

"I could have killed him."

"Then what you say is true, you would never have had me. I came to you only because you told me you wanted to kill him. That's what you told me in the crowd in the chapel, when you were crushing my arms. "Say, what is that moon on your right arm?" "It's a vaccination. Oh, answer me! You must keep your promise."

"You're free, gringa. Vaccination?"

"Did you mean for me to discover love without loving? That isn't a woman's true freedom. You're mistaken."

And again he asked: You didn't like it, gringuita? Tell me you liked it, with or without a promise, you do like it, yes? and you want more, my precious gringuita, sweet gringa, my beautiful, loving little gringa, really making love for the first time, vaccination and all, tell me, didn't you love our lovemaking, gringuita?"

"Yes!"

And this is what Harriet Winslow never forgave Tomás Arroyo.

[123]

**16**

You know why I came back? he asked Harriet Winslow, then did not ask but stated: You *know* why I came back. Your eyes are running away from you, gringuita, you must be fleeing from something if you want so much to return to it: look, you saw yourself in the mirror, you think I don't know? I saw myself in the mirrors, too, when I was a little boy; but my men had never seen their full bodies: I had to give them that big gift, that fiesta, to say to them: Now, see yourselves, move, raise an arm, dance a polka, make up for all the years you lived blindly with your own bodies, groping in the dark for a body—your own—as strange and silent and distant as all the other bodies that you were not allowed to touch. Or that were not allowed to touch you. They moved in front of a mirror and broke my spell, my enchantment, gringuita. You know, there is a children's game here. It is called "the enchanted." Anyone who touches you enchants you. You must remain frozen until someone else comes to touch you. Then you can move again. Who can say how long it will be before someone else enchants you once more? It is a dangerous word. You are bedazzled. But you do not own yourself anymore. You belong to someone else who can be good or bad to you, who knows? Listen, gringuita: I have been enchanted by this house since I was born here, not in my father's plush canopied bed, but on a straw *petate* in the servants' quarters. The hacienda and I have faced one another for thirty years, as you faced a a mirror, as my men saw themselves reflected. I was paralyzed by stone and adobe and tile and glass and porcelain and wood. A house is all that, but much more than that, too. Did you have a house you could call your own when you were a girl, gringuita? Or did you also look at a house that could have been yours, that somehow was yours, you know?, but was more distant than a palace in a fairy tale. Some things are both yours and not yours; they are painfully yours because they are *not* yours. You understand? You see another house, perhaps you understand that house: you see the lights go on and scurry from window to window, then you see them flicker out at night, and you are inside the house but also outside the house, angry because you are excluded but grateful that you can see the house, while they, the others, the rest, the many, many, are inside, captive, and cannot see. Then they become the excluded, and you exult, gringuita, you are happy and there is a fiesta in your heart: you have two houses and they have only one.

Arroyo let out a ghastly sigh, more like the groan of someone kicked in the groin, and concealed his involuntary expulsion of inner passions with a clearing of the throat, a rough spitting of thick phlegm into a cup of mescal. It was an ugly sight and Harriet hid from it, but he grabbed her chin firmly.

"Look at me," said Arroyo, naked in front of Harriet, kneeling naked with his brown hard chest and deep navel and uneasy sex, never restful, she found out, always half full, like the bottle of mescal he always left sitting around anyplace he was, as if the hard long testicles like a pair of furry avocados swinging but hard as stones between his slim, sleek, hairless Indian thighs were constantly in the act of refilling that fat, heaving penis, sleek again, crowned by an aureola of the blackest hair she had ever seen (and she laughed, thinking of Delaney's scraggly, reddish, sparse pubic hair, which she had seen only once, through a half-opened fly, like some dismal dwarf in a laundry shop, but felt so many times, when he asked her,

Be my woman, Harriet, prove your love to me, do what I like, you know, no danger for you, sweetheart, only your soft little hand, Harriet: and his jerky, cold little pleasures). Arroyo was like an even, fluid stream of sex: that is what his name meant, Brook, Stream, Creek: Tom Creek, Tom Brook, what a good English name for a man who looked like Tomás Arroyo! She laughed with him kneeling there in front of her, not flaunting his perpetual semi-erection, which she saw and touched wistfully, understanding that there was nothing to be understood in it, that Arroyo, her Tom Brook, was the quintessentially uncomplicated stud: she had heard it said that men such as cattle drivers, sheep shearers, construction workers, always had a hard-on handy, they were not complicated by thoughts about sex, they used it as normally as they walked, sneezed, slept, or ate—was Arroyo like this? She thought so for a moment, then hated herself for patronizing him once more. How much better to think that Arroyo's cock was always ready, or half ready, really, thanks to a complicated imagination that she had no way of truly fathoming: perhaps he was like this only with her, not with other women?

"Harriet Winslow," she silently remonstrated with herself. "Pride is a sin. Don't you become a silly infatuated lass at this late hour. You are not driving anyone wild, in Mexico or in Washington. Hush, baby, hush, Miss Harriet, steady now."

She was not talking to herself then; her own imagination had taken her into the arms of her father's lover, the damp black woman in the damp hushed mansion where the lights moved up and down the stairs.

"Look at me," Arroyo repeated, look at me facing you (this is what he wanted to say, anyway, she thought; now

[126]

she sits alone and remembers), unable to move while I face you, because you are beautiful, perhaps, but beauty is not the only reason to remain like this, transfixed in front of someone or something: a snake—she grinned— for example, or a mirage in the desert; or a nightmare from which you cannot escape, falling forever into the shaft of sleep, running forever out of your own sleep; no, said Arroyo, you think sad and ugly things, gringa, I mean beauty, or love, or because I suddenly remember who you are or you make me remember who I am, or maybe we remember somebody each on his own but are grateful to the person we are face to face with for bringing that sweet memory back to us; yes—she held up the palm of her hand—I can imagine many things that never were here tonight, or desire that we never had, said Arroyo, placing his palm against hers: she cold and dry, he hot and dry too, both kneeling, their knees churning up a froth of sheets, the bed like a still surf which would come to life as soon as the train moved once more, hurried on to its next encounter, the battle, the campaign, whatever came next in Arroyo's life. Then the bed of the Mirandas where they were kneeling together in love would heave on its own, unmindful of the bodies that now gave it its only rhythm: a sea of slow cool tides and sudden flashes of heat from the unsuspected depths where an octopus could move in senseless fear and clouds of black sand would funnel upward, warming the waters with the suddenly revealed fever of the unmoving, breaking the mirrors of the cool sea, splintering the surface of reality.

Each closed his fists over the other's.

He said that he had been as if mesmerized for nearly thirty years, as a child, and a boy, and a young man of the hacienda. Then there had been this stirring. He had not started it. He had simply joined it. He did understand that it was his, as if he had fathered the Revolution, in the loins of the desert of Chihuahua, yes, gringuita, just like that. But that was not the important thing. The thing was that he had moved, at last, he and all of them, stirring, heaving, rising as if from a drugged sleep—slow, brown, parched, and wounded animals, rising from the bed of the desert, the hollow of the mountain, the naked feet of the little flea-bitten villages, had she talked to La Luna, the moon-faced woman, who had come from a little town in northern Mexico, did she know? Well, he had thrilled to that movement, and now, and now—he struck down her hand in his and held it over his uneasy cock—and now he would only say it to her, he would never tell La Luna, she would understand but feel betrayed because they were both Mexicans, now he would tell the gringa, because he could tell it only to someone from a land as far away and strange as the United States, the Other World, the world that is not Mexico, the foreign and distant and curious, eccentric, marginal world of the Yankees who did not enjoy good food or violent revolution or women in bondage, or beautiful churches, and broke with all tradition just for the sake of it, as if there were good things only in the future and in novelty; he was able to tell the gringa this not only because she was different but because now they, the Mexicans, were, for an instant only, perhaps like her, like the old gringo, like all of them, restless, moving, forgetting their ancient fealty to one place and one landscape and one graveyard.

This he would tell her: "Gringa, I am locked in again."

"What do you mean?" she asked, startled once more by this man whose words were her surprise.

"I mean this. Understand me. Try. I was paralyzed

when facing the hacienda, as if it was my own ghost. Then I broke out and moved. Now I am paralyzed again."

"Because you came back here?" She tried to be kind.

"No, no, no." He shook his head vigorously. "More than that. I am once more a prisoner of what I am doing. As if I weren't moving at all again."

He was locked into the destiny of the Revolution, where she had surprised him, he wanted to say. No, it was more than coming back to the hacienda. Much more than that—he let his head fall on Harriet's naked thighs: We all have dreams, but when our dreams become our fate, should we be happy that they've come true?

He didn't know. Neither did she. But Harriet did start to think then that perhaps this man had been able to do what no one was supposed to: he had come home again, he was trying to relive one of the oldest myths of mankind, the return to the lar, the earth, the warm home of our origins.

That cannot be done, she told herself, and not only because very likely the place won't be there anymore. Even if it were, though, nothing could ever be the same: people age, things break down, feelings change. You can never go home again, even to the same place and the same people, if by chance both have remained, not the same, but simply *there*, in their essence. She realized that the English language could only conjugate one kind of being —*to be*. Home is a memory. The only true memory: for memory is our home. And thus the only true desire of our hearts: the burning quest for our tiny, insecure paradises, buried deep within our hearts, impervious to poverty or wealth, kindness or cruelty. A glowing nugget of self-awareness which will only shine for the child? she asked.

No, he answered intuitively, a child is but a witness. I

was the witness of the hacienda. Because I was the bastard in the servants' quarters, I was forced to imagine what *they* took for granted. I grew up smelling, breathing, hearing every single room, every single corner of this house. I could know without moving, without opening my eyes, you see, gringuita? I could breathe with the place and see what each one was doing in his own bedroom, in his bathroom, in the dining room, there was nothing either secret or public for me the little witness, Harriet, I who saw them all, heard them all, imagined and smelled them all by simply breathing with the rhythm they didn't possess because they didn't need it, they took it all for granted, I had to breathe in the hacienda, fill my lungs with its smallest flake of paint, and be the absent witness to every single copulation, hurried or languorous, imaginative or boring, whining or proud, tender or cold, to every single defecation, thick or watery, green or red, smooth or caked with undigested corn, I heard every fart, do you hear, every belch, every spit fall, every pee run, and I saw the scrawny turkeys having their necks twisted, the oxen emasculated, the goats eviscerated and put on the spit, I saw the bottles being corked full of the uneasy wine of the Coahuila valleys, so near to the desert that they taste like cactus wine, then the medicine bottles being uncorked for the castor-oil purges, and the fevers running high in death and childbirth and children's diseases, I could touch the red velvets and creamy organdies and green taffetas of the hoopskirts and bonnets of the ladies, their long lace nightgowns with the Sacred Heart of Jesus embroidered in front of their cunts: the quivering, humble devotion to the votive lamps quietly sweating away their orange-colored wax as if caught up in a perpetual holy orgasm; contrasting, gringa, with the chandeliers of the vast mansion of stylish, expensive wooden floors and heavy draperies and golden tassels and grandfather clocks and wingtip chairs and rickety dining-room chairs bathed in golden paint—I saw it all, and then one day my old friend, the most ancient man in the hacienda, a man maybe as old as the hacienda itself, a man who had never worn shoes and did not make noise (Graciano his name was, now I recall it), dressed in white peasant shirt and pants, a piece of rawhide that man, wearing clothes that had been patched over and over again till it was impossible to distinguish between the patches on his clothes and the wrinkles on his skin, as if the body also had been patched over a thousand times: Graciano with his white stubble on head and chin was the old man charged with winding the clocks every evening, and one night he took me with him.

I did not ask him. He just took me by the hand and when we reached the clock in the sitting room where they were all having coffee and brandy after dinner, Graciano gave me the keys to the house. He was the only man in the servants' quarters who was entrusted with them. And he gave them to me that night to hold as he wound the big grandfather clock in the vestibule to the sitting room.

Gringa: I held these keys in my hand for one instant. They were hot and cold, as if the keys, too, spoke of the life and death of the rooms they opened.

I tried to imagine the rooms the hot keys would open; and which, the cold keys.

It was just an instant.

I clutched the keys as though clutching the whole house. The house was in my power during that instant. They were all in my power. They must have sensed it, because (I am sure) for the first time in anyone's life they stopped their chatter and their drinking and smoking and looked toward the old man winding the clock, and a beautiful lady in green saw me and came up to me, knelt in front of me, and said: "How cute!"

The young lady's appreciation of my nine-year-old cuteness was not shared by the rest of the company. I saw huddled movements, heard low voices, then an embarrassed silence as the young lady looked back as if to share her delight with them, but only met icy stares, then asked in silence, "What have I done now?" She was the young bride of the eldest son of my father. She was the mother of the children, my nephews, that you came to teach English to, gringa. She had yet, twenty years ago, to understand the ways of the Mirandas. I stared, clutching the keys to the house.

Then the man who was my father barked: "Graciano, take those keys from the brat."

The old man held out his hand, asking for his gift back.

I understood don Graciano. I gave him the keys, letting him know that now that I had had them in my hands, now I understood that he had made me this wonderful gift for some reason unknown. When I gave back the keys, they were hot, but my hand was cold.

Then don Graciano took me with him to his bunk in the servants' quarters and he just sat there with a distant look that I have later come to recognize in the eyes of those who are about to depart but do not know it yet. Sometimes when we see them, we know before they do who is going, and when. There is distance in the eyes, an inward gaze says: "Look at me. I'm going. I don't know it yet. But that is because I'm looking at myself within myself, and not outside myself. You who see me from the outside, tell me if I'm not right, and look here, fellow, don't let me die all alone."

Of course, don Graciano did not speak of this, but rather of other things that night. He said, I remember (Arroyo remembered), that many times the owners wanted to pass their worn-out city clothes to him, thus honoring him and showing their esteem. He counseled me never to accept such hand-me-downs. He told me to wear my work clothes always. He said it that night. He spoke of charity and how much he hated it. He spoke of speaking, of talking like we talk, not parroting the speech of the owners. He said never to explain anything; better suffer lashes than complain or explain. If you had to survive, better do so without even saying "I didn't mean to," or "I don't feel well." He held me close to him and his heartbeat was fainter than that of the little desert lizards I sometimes caught fleeing a crumbling corner of the servants' quarters.

Charity, he said, is the enemy of dignity—it's not pride that's a sin, he said, pride is simply dignity. Pride is not a right, he said, scratching under the rolled-up woolen *jorongo* that served for him to rest his head on, for pride is not a right. Dignity is. He produced a beautiful flat case of rosewood, gringa, hidden there in his artfully rolled-up *jorongo*, saying that dignity was a right, and the right was right here in this box: he had given me the keys but had to take them back or they would know that something was up. But what was inside this wooden box he could leave with me, since they did not know about it but I should, since I was the true heir to the Miranda estate.

I took the box, full of wonder, not truly understanding anything, just full of awe at what was happening to me this day, but assuring don Graciano that I would protect that little box as if it were my own life.

He nodded, smiling. "Our forebears will come to my burial and receive me because I have held the papers in trust."

That is all he said. He said nothing more.

Then he heaved a big sigh and patted my head and told me to go to bed and come see him the next day.

I swear to you, Harriet, he did not say, We will talk tomorrow; he did not say, Be sure to come tomorrow so that we can talk some more. He certainly did not say, Listen, Tomasito, I'm going to die and I want you to be here with me, so don't fail me tomorrow. No, gringa, he did not say, Listen, Tomás, stay with me, stay by my cot tonight and watch me die: I want you to see me die; you owe me that for taking you into the house and having you see them and having them see you, not the way they like, amid the huddled multitudes, you know, they are delighted not to acknowledge anyone, they look right over you as if you weren't there, and I wanted to tell them: Here he is. You can't see through Tomás Arroyo. He is not air, he is blood. He is flesh, not glass. He is not transparent. He is opaque, you damn bunch of prissy motherfuckers, he is as solid as the thickest wall of a prison you or I or he are ever likely to be in.

This was Graciano's farewell to his years and years at the Miranda hacienda.

Next day, he was found dead on his cot. I saw him as they took him out to bury. "It is Graciano," they said. "We wonder who is going to wind the clocks now."

He was old too, Harriet, like your old gringo. He was buried here in the same desert that the Indiana General found when he came. But when he was buried, all our forefathers were at the gathering, you know, the Apaches and Tobosos and Laguneros who roamed the land when it had no owner, who hunted and killed there, and also the Spaniards, who came with a hunger for the golden cities of this desert, as they thought, and those who came with the cross after them, when they found there was no gold, and finally those who came to settle the land and drive claims into it with their silver spikes and their iron spurs, taking the land from the Indians, who came back shooting and raping and pounding the hoofs of their newfound stallions over the desert, and who were killed, or shipped off to prisons in the tropics where they would die of evil fevers, or went up the mountains, farther up each time, until they disappeared like the smoke you sometimes see on the very crown of the tallest peaks, as though this were their daily offering to the death we owe ourselves and others each day: a gray column of haze leaving this world, saying we are glad to part with something every day, even if it's just a puff of cloudy sky, so that when we do go for good we will be used to it, we will recognize ourselves in our death that preceded us, gringuita, do you see my death as part of my life?

No, she said, life is one thing and death is another: they are opposites, enemies, and we should not combine them lest we cease to safeguard life, which is brittle and can cease to be at any moment. Ah, then it does contain its own death, pounced Arroyo. No, no—Harriet shook her loose tresses—life is surrounded by its enemy; we are besieged by what denies us: sin and death, the devil, the other. She dropped her gaze and added: But we can be saved by good works and personal decency, abstinences —she looked askance at the ubiquitous bottle of mescal, then chided herself for her lack of charity—and the

Lord's grace, which is ever-present, available to us because it is abundant and that is why He is the Lord. Arroyo looked hard at her because in her eyes a moment before she dropped them he could discover nothing that turned her words into truth: they were only convictions, and that is not the same, but should he respect them?

"You know what, gringuita? Don Graciano lived a very long time."

"I hope the old American also lives out his allotted time."

"Allotted time!" exclaimed Arroyo, and then laughed, laying his head on her mound. "Let him live just as much as he has lived up until now, let him double his life, gringuita, and you will see how he will hate it. He will hate us if we grant it to him. No, gringa, we die because our paths cross. The desert is big. Graciano, don Graciano, was buried in it. He always lived here. His forefathers came to see him being laid in the ground. The old gringo came here. No one asked him. He has no forebears here. It would be a lonely death. No one would visit his grave. It would have no name. Tell him to go away quick, gringa. He is not one of us. He does not believe in the Revolution. He believes in death. I fear him, gringa. He has no forebears in this desert."

Tell me about yours, she pleaded, feeling that after the closeness of an instant, separation had crept in, and she wanted the closeness to last while it could; she was certain, if not of the fellowship or enmity of life and death, that, in life itself, being separated was the common lot, not being together; and being separate, she told Arroyo softly, that was death in life, didn't he think so?

He answered by picking up his narrative, saying that the white men first, then the mestizos that soon populated the land, they too suffered like the Indians; they too lost their small holdings to the encroaching haciendas, the large properties financed from abroad or from Mexico City, making instant swells of all those who had the money to buy up the lands at auction when they were pried from the priests; and the small landholders, like his own people, again were left in the lurch of history. Take to the hills, little Arroyo, live with the Indians and become a puff of smoke, or crawl the desert during the day like a lizard, hiding in the shadows of the giant cacti, and strike at night like a wolf, running across the dry, orphaned ocean, or become a laborer here in the hacienda: maybe if you behave you will be given the keys again, you can wind the clocks in your old age, Tomás, preserve your dignity by refusing hand-me-down clothes. Pass me the beans, will you?

"I have come back to destroy that destiny, you understand?" He looked up at Harriet and their eyes met upside down, strange marine-life eyes accentuated by eyebrows like bags, mustaches, stray pubic jokes, yet his tone was so severe, so implacable, that she could not find anything funny in it: "I have come back so that no one ever again has the choice that was mine in Mexico."

She thought how the old gringo would laugh at such an assertion, and why wasn't she laughing, too, or wasn't irritated anymore as she'd been at the start, when they met and she would not call him General? Why? Why? She searched her soul and found a searing heat there; but it was the heat of smoldering ashes, a dying fire, which is the hottest, most resilient fire of them all. Was it Arroyo's fire, too, or was it—she now shut her eyes quickly so as not to see those two swimming porpoises that were Arroyo's eyes—truly her own fire, saved for her own grace

[137]

after Arroyo had kindled it, but not his, no, his only momentarily, he the instrument for reviving a fire that had always been there but that was hers, that belonged to the fall of the house of Halston, to summers never seen on the Sound and to her mother and her father and her father's black woman, a fire that belonged to all of this, a fire which was hers and which he now wanted to attribute to himself, with macho petulance and unrelenting theatricality. She saw him now once more in his unlearned, spontaneous poses, a bullfighter in a vacant ring at night, surrounded by the dead smell of carcasses, an unsuspecting tenor in one of the Italian operas she had seen with her mother at the National Theater, but again, deprived of decor, costumes, heavy brocaded curtains: a naked singer, oh, a child almost, in his uneasy, rising, half-grown way. She did what she had never done in all her life, she swooped like a fragile but hungry bird down between his loins, she took that uneasy, rising, half-grown thing between her lips, she smelled at last the strange seed, she licked it off the arrow's tip, she bit, she sucked, she swallowed what had been inside her, but now as though, by this act, she were inside him, as though, before, she had been possessed by him and now he were possessed by her: that was the difference, now she felt she could bite it off if she wished, and before he had been able to thrust like a sword and cut her in half, come out beyond her, piercing her like a butterfly; before, she could have been his victim, and now he could be hers; and so Arroyo now grew but refused to come, damn him, damn the brown fucker, damn the ugly greaser, he refused because he wanted to strangle her, suffocate her, pounding, heaving, thrusting, refusing to spill into her mouth, refusing to cry as he did with the moon-faced woman, damn him, refusing to shrink and be beaten, refusing to acknowledge that in her mouth he was her captive, but again making her feel that she would throttle first before he ever came and shrank and let her savor victory.

She rejected him with a savage, guttural sound, the worst sound that she had ever felt herself emit, as she spit out that hard rattlesnake which bit her lips and beat against her cheeks, flapping as she screamed what is it with you, what makes you what you are, you damned brown prick, what makes you refuse a woman a moment as free and powerful as the one you took before?

And, for this, Harriet Winslow never forgave him.

17 The old man is plodding along in a straight line, muttering to himself stories he had once written, cruel stories of the American Civil War in which men succumb and survive because they have been granted a fragmented consciousness: because a man can be at once dying—hanging from a bridge with a rope around his neck—and watching his death from the far side of the creek: because a man can dream of a horseman and kill his own father, all in the same instant.

The roving, ranging consciousness disperses itself like pollen on a spring day; the same thing that shatters it also saves it. But along with this splintered consciousness of the universe, one question travels with us through life, asking: What is the strongest pretext for loving?

Although Harriet was walking beside the old gringo he continued muttering, not caring whether she heard or understood him. If it is necessary, our atomized consciousness invents love, imagines it or feigns it, but does not live without it, since in the midst of infinite dispersion, love, even if as a pretext, gives us the measure of our loss.

The time comes to renounce even the pretext; he had written: "The time to quit is when you have lost a big stake, your fool hope of eventual success, your fortitude, and your love of the game."

He looked at her, walking beside him now, matching him stride for stride, capable of keeping step with the gringo, a long, silent step unlike the quick, staccato, clicking heels of the children of the Spanish world. He looked at her, this agile, sure, elegant thirty-one-year-old woman who reminded him of his daughter, and his wife when she was young. She was following him closely so they could both watch Arroyo, energetic and active on the distant, dusty plain, haranguing, perhaps destroying what Harriet Winslow had so delicately constructed. She was following him closely and finally understood his words: he had you as if you were an object; you let yourself be violated by the animal appetite of that man; he took you to satisfy his arrogance and his vanity, nothing more.

"No. He didn't have me. I had him."

The old gringo stopped and for the first time looked at her with real fury. His bitter blue eyes seemed as sad as his words, but his eyes belied the words: they were truly violent. "Then, Harriet, it was you who was lonely and hungry."

He meant: you didn't need to be alone, because ever since I met you, you've been living a second life, you have been loved without knowing it, in the thousand fragments of my feelings and my dreams. Even in the mirrors of the ballroom, which you entered without vanity as if into a forgotten dream, even there, without knowing, you were living and being loved.

"No," Harriet replied. "I didn't take him for the reason you think, because I know I could have found consolation elsewhere."

He didn't blink. She hadn't heard his thoughts. The bitter blue gaze didn't flinch.

"Then why, for God's sake, why?"

"He said he was going to kill you. I told him he could have me if that would save your life."

The old man did not react immediately; it took him several minutes to absorb her words before bursting into laughter, bellowing laughter with tears running down his face, doubled over as if bowed by the alkaline wind that robbed him of breath. She stood watching, uncomprehending, filling the space of his laughter with more justifications, a spate of words: Arroyo said he could have killed you that night, when you disobeyed him and refused to kill the Colonel; he said that was reason enough; you rebelled against him, your superior; you asked to join Arroyo's troops, he didn't invite you; he thought you were trying to win his confidence and couldn't understand why you would rather prove it by tossing a silver peso in the air than by killing a Federal colonel. I said to him: "You say the Colonel died like a brave man. Wouldn't that have been enough?" "No," he told me. "I could also have told you the old man died like a coward." "Why, why did you have to tell me this?"

"Because I saw him kiss you the other night. I saw him. I saw him with you in your bedroom, and another time, and another. It is not very nice, I'm sorry. I learned to spy as a child. My father was a rich landowner. I spied on him as he was drinking and fornicating, not knowing his son was watching him, waiting for the moment to kill him. But I didn't kill him. My father got away. And now the defiant gringo is getting away because we both know you would never make love to a murderer."

"I swear I made my decision to come to Mexico before they jailed Mr. Delaney for federal fr—"

"A check for seventy-five million dollars, made out to the Treasury of the United States, Mr. Stan—"

"I don't want President Díaz touched with so much as a rose petal; our boss, Mr. Hearst, has too many interests in Mex—"

" 'Was there anybody on the horse?' 'Yes, my father.' 'Good God!' "

"He never returned from Cuba. Missing in action. An empty grave. Good God!"

"I spied on him drinking and fornicating. He got away from me. Good God!"

The old gringo stopped laughing and began to cough, a deep, racking cough.

"You have been deceived from the beginning," he said, with difficulty, wondering whether they, the two gringos, could at last bring their true emotions into the light without killing them the way flowers wilt at the touch of sun and air when they are removed from the shaded nooks where they grow. "First, the Mirandas brought you here to help them avoid suspicion and escape more easily. The Capetians of France might have saved their skins if they'd thought to engage a teacher the very night of their flight. But this isn't Varennes, Harriet. And now you've been convinced that by giving your body to the General you would save my life."

Again the old man exploded into bitter laughter. "Rich

or poor, the Mexicans always get the best of us. They hate us. We're the gringos. Their eternal enemies."

"I don't understand," said Harriet, confused and unbelieving. "He was really going to kill you."

"Did he say why?"

"Because a man who has no fear is a danger to his comrades and to his enemies. I think that's what he said. Because sometimes there is a courage worse than fear."

"No. The real reason."

He meant to say, her reason, her own reason, imagining her captive and liberated by her own past, the dreamed past, the humid tidewater summers, the light in the old house, her father, the black woman, the lamp on her mother's table, the solitude and happiness when her father went away and never returned, a forty-two-year-old beau who asked, Aren't you happy? You are my ideal woman.

"You're right. He also said he was jealous."

The old man had begun walking again, mulling over the events of the hour, but when Harriet said this, he paused, then gathered her into his arms and pressed her head to his breast.

"Oh, child, my poor, beautiful child," said the old gringo, fighting the emotion he had felt ever since she told him Arroyo had wanted to kill him and she had given herself to save him. "Oh, my beautiful little girl. You haven't saved me from anything."

Then the roving consciousness that was the seal and fascination of his imagination, if not his genius, asked the old gringo: Did you know she has been creating you just as you were creating her? Did you know, old man, that she had created a plan for living for you? Did you know we are all the object of another's imagination?

"Don't you understand? I want to die. That's why I came here. To be killed."

Huddled against the old man's breast, Harriet smelled the fresh lotion on his shirt; she lifted a loving hand and stroked the old man's lean, clean-shaven cheeks, free for once of the customary white stubble. He was a handsome old man. It frightened her, suddenly, to realize he was clean, shaved, perfumed, as if in preparation for some great ceremony. But she was unexpectedly distracted by the distant commotion in the village. Arroyo was speaking to the people, moving rapidly and with authority among them. The gringos were watching from a distance, but they saw him in close detail: cruel and tender, just and unjust, vigilant and lax, resentful and self-confident, active and lazy, modest and arrogant: the quintessential Latin Indian. They watched him as they stood in an embrace, immersed in odors and deceits, silhouetted against the setting sun, far from their own cities and rivers, subjugated by the feeling of revelation that "like the face of God in the desert" comes but once or twice in a lifetime.

The old man whispered quickly in her ear: "I will never kill myself, because that is how my son died and I don't want to duplicate his pain."

He told her he had no right to complain, much less to seek compassion now that misfortune had come to him. He had no right because he had mocked the unhappiness of others; he had spent his life accusing people of being unhappy. He had surrounded his family with a hatred alien to them.

"Maybe my children are the proof that I didn't hate the whole universe. But they hated me, anyway."

She listened to him, but said only that life was worth

living and that she would prove it to him; there was a child in the village, a two-year-old baby girl . . . But the old gringo was holding her away, saying that he already knew, that as soon as he entered Mexico his senses had been awakened. Crossing the mountains and the desert, he felt that he could hear and smell and taste and see as never before, as if he were young again, better than young again—he smiled—when lack of experience had prevented comparisons, and now he felt liberated from the filthy editorial rooms and the yellow lamplighted parlors, and the stinking barrooms where his son had died and his life had stagnated while all the dead of California lifted their whiskey glasses in a toast to the imminent earthquake and the imminent disappearance of El Dorado into the sea, forever, and to the good fortune of humankind: liberated from Hearst, liberated from the young parenticides who circle around a famous writer like the ubiquitous buzzards of Mexico, and leaving those who admired him not the memory of a decrepit old man but the suspicion of a horseman in the sky.

"I want to be a good-looking corpse." The blue eyes sparked.

"To be a gringo in Mexico . . . ah, that is euthanasia."

Here, now, amid the copper-colored mountains and the shimmering, translucent evening and the odors of tortillas and chilis, and the distant guitars, as Arroyo was swallowed up in the cage of mirrors of the ballroom he had saved from destruction, he could listen and taste and smell almost supernaturally, like the man hanged from Owl Creek Bridge, who at the instant of his death could see the veining of each leaf; more: the very insects upon them; more: the prismatic colors in all the dewdrops upon a million blades of grass.

His ranging consciousness, close to final unity, told him that this was the great compensation for the loves he had lost because he deserved to lose them. Mexico had, instead, compensated him with a life: the life of his senses, awakened from lethargy by his proximity to death, the dignity of nature as the last joy of his life: would she corrupt all this by offering him the body that last night had belonged to Arroyo?

"I had a final vanity," said the old gringo, smiling. "I wanted to be killed by Pancho Villa himself. This is what I meant when I wrote a farewell note to a dear friend, a woman poet, saying: You won't see me again; you may hear of me being stood up against a Mexican stone wall and shot to rags. It beats falling down the cellar stairs."

He stood looking into Harriet's gray eyes. He let the minute expand in silence, gravely, so they could feel it to the fullest.

"I am afraid of falling in love with you," he told her, as if these were the first words he had ever spoken. She had been the final answer to the mad dream of the artist with a split consciousness. She had seen the books in his open suitcase. She knew that he had brought the *Quixote* but not that he wanted to read it before he died. She saw the scribbled papers and stubby pencils. Maybe she knew that nothing is seen until the writer names it. Language permits us to see. Without the word, we are all blind. He kissed her, he kissed her like a lover, like a man, not with Arroyo's sensuality, but with a shared covetousness.

"Don't you know I wanted to save you in order to save my own father from a second death?" she asked, with an urgency punctuated by her new awareness. "Don't you know that with Arroyo I could be like my father, free, and sensual, but that in you I have a father. Don't you know that?"

"Yes!" he said. "Yes!" as she had said to Arroyo when Arroyo had made her feel like a whore and she had reveled in being what she despised. He tried to hold her apart, only to assure himself that there were tears in those beautiful eyes, but quickly pressed her to his breast again, blinding her, so he could say what he had to say now that he thought he knew everything, and knowing everything was to know there was something still to know. She had changed forever, her embrace told him that, her warmth, the nearness of this beautiful woman who could be his wife or his daughter but was neither, only herself, at last. He had been the privileged witness to the moment when a person, man or woman, changes forever, clings fatefully to the instant for which he or she was born and then lets it go, without yearning but with sadness. She had changed forever; his daughter changed in the arms and between the legs of his son, and nothing he could invent, no mockery, no accusation, no devil's dictionary, could prevent it. All that was left was to accept the change Harriet had undergone in Arroyo's violent love, and demand something of her in the name of the love that could not be, the love between the old man readying himself for death and the young girl who had come alive: "Now, tell me the truth, by whatever is holy to you; don't let me leave without hearing your secret."

(She sits alone, and remembers. My lover. My daughter.)

"All right. My father did not die in combat. He was bored with us and stayed in Cuba to live with a Negress. But we told everyone he was dead and we collected the pension in order to live. He wrote me in secret, asking me to understand. What could I understand, when I didn't know how to feel? He didn't say it, but we killed him, my mother and I, in order to live. The worst was that I never knew whether she knew what I knew or whether she cashed the monthly check in good faith. I tell you, I didn't want to understand; I wanted to feel . . ."

To bring skin and sensation and movement to life, to make them one. No one understood her. Did he understand her? The old man nodded. She swore that although she knew who he was, she would never tell anyone. That would be her way of loving him from now on.

"I shall forget your real name."

"Thank you," the old gringo said simply, and added that he regretted she had come to offer life and instead must stay to witness death.

"You mean, although I came to teach, I am the one who is being taught," she said, wiping her eyes and nose on her full sleeve, following the old gringo now, faithful, from this moment his vestal virgin, sanctifying those minutes when they succeeded in uniting—each in the other's—their split consciousness, before the final dispersion they sensed was near: time, Mexico, war, memory, flesh itself, had given them more time than most men and women are allowed.

"Maybe," the old man said. "We all try to be virtuous. It's our national pastime."

"You want me to tell you I didn't go to bed with Arroyo to save your life and to feel virtuous, but because I wanted his body, and that I enjoyed it."

"Yes, I would like that. Even though our other national pastime is to tell the truth, we can't keep a secret. That, too, to feel virtuous, of course. Washington, as a boy, could not deny he had chopped down the cherry tree. I think young Juárez was able to hide that he had designs on his master's precious daughter."

"I liked it," Harriet said, oblivious to what he was saying.

She said she liked the way he loved (he heard it and attributed her pleasure to himself, to his old body); she wanted him to know. "I also want you to know that Tomás Arroyo had no right to my body and that I will make him pay for it."

Harriet looked at the old gringo exactly as he wanted to be looked at before he died. He felt that her gaze completed the fragmented sequence of his imagination of Harriet Winslow that had begun in the reflections of the mirrors in the ballroom that was but a threshold of the road to dream, atomized into a thousand oneiric instants and now joined again in the words that told the old gringo that Harriet would not allow a living testimony to her sensuality, that she was giving the old man the right to dream about her, but not Arroyo.

 The moon-faced woman wound the phonograph player and stealthily put the needle on the twirling record. Out of the loudspeaker, shaped like a ribbed beige cornucopia (thought Harriet) and adorned with the figure of a little black-and-white dog listening to His Master's Voice, came the soothing yet jarring sound of Nora Bayes singing "By the light of the silvery moon."

By the light light light of the . . .

[149]

Harriet thought of the Wabash and the other languorous rivers of North America, then refused to look out through the windows of the stalled train at the Mexican desert.

The woman did not say it, but her hushed voice let her understand that the scratchy music was meant to muffle her words: this was a woman perpetually fearful of being overheard by men, Harriet thought with a certain scorn.

The tinny church bell of the hacienda rang out.

The woman called La Luna said it was strange to hear a bell and not recognize the reason for its sound. That's how she knew the Revolution had arrived at her small provincial town in Durango: the bells started ringing at a time no one could call vespers or matins or anything else. It was like a new time, she said, a time we could not imagine, and then she thought of the regularity of our time, generation after generation abiding by the traditional seasons, the traditional hours, even the traditional minutes; she had been brought up that way, decent, not too wealthy but with enough to be well-off, her father a grain merchant, her husband a moneylender in that same little town where, child or woman, you got up at five, so you could dress while it was still dark (that was extremely important, not to see your own body ever), then be at church at six in the morning and walk back hungry even if you had swallowed the body of Christ (the mystery that enlivened her memories, the mystery that teased her imagination: a body in a piece of bread, the body of a man born from a woman who had never known man's flesh, you know, Miss Winslow, we speak in terrible circumlocutions here, we were taught as girls never to say *legs*, but that's what I walk on, never *buttocks*, but that's what I sit on—she laughed softly, almost sighing; the body of a man who was God, the body of a man who shared his Godliness with two other men; she imagined them as men: a second bearded man, old and mighty, sitting on a throne, who was at the same time the young man nailed to the cross; and a third, spectral, ageless man, a magician who called himself a Ghost, and Holy at that, and who was surely responsible in her childish imagination for all the other transformations: one into three, three into one, one into the virgin, then out of the same virgin, then dead, then resurrected and presumably back into three without ceasing to be one and then three-into-one into wafer, many, many millions of tiny pieces of bread all containing Him, and the Magician working away, the Ghost of a Spectral World). The church thus became a specter, as did my own home, as did my destiny; we were all specters wandering around in shifts—breakfast, then lessons, in what was known as home economy, then lunch, then cake making, then prayers, then dinner, then a little piano, then to undress in the dark and go to bed: like a child, and you'll say it wasn't bad. But when the life of a man was yoked unto the life of a child bride, Miss Harriet, then that life became dark, repetitive, as things are when they come to a standstill and do not blossom forth from what they were before, before the man, the father, the husband, was there to see to it that you remained a child bride, that marriage was a ceremony of fear: fear that you might be punished for not being a little girl anymore; yet this man takes you, señorita, and punishes you with his sex for not being a little girl anymore, for betraying him with your sexual blood and your sexual hair, and I who soon proved barren was for that reason worse—there was no justification for my ugly hairy mound, my fierce hairy armpits, my abundant, sewer-like menstruations, my irritated, inflated, blooming but milk-less nipples. He draped me in long coarse thick night-gowns with a slit in front of my cunt and the Sacred Heart of Jesus embroidered there in thick, red, silvery thread, a frozen emblem of my dirty womanhood, holy now in this blind encounter with his own untouchable sex: a quick thrust, a heavy sigh, a few seconds; I knew that he mastur-bated many times so as to avoid me, and when his imagi-nation dried up or he needed me to prove his manliness to himself, even then he would play with himself first, so as to be instantly ready to thrust it in, let it come and swiftly withdraw it. I was not to have any pleasure, and I refused to, with him or without him; I betrayed all my teachings and saw myself a few times in front of a mirror, but then did not do it anymore, not because I was tempted to let my fingers wander down from my flourish-ing nipples to my heavy dark crotch, but because I started seeing myself in that mirror as an ancient child, a silly crone muttering childish babble, a ruined doll singing obscene nursery rhymes and sticking the imaginary dicks of stuffed animals into my withered, prune-like vagina— bells, matins, vespers, confessions, communions, Hail Marys, mea culpas, Credos, thick holy smoke in church and out of it, homilies, fear of Hell, love of Jesus, love of Jesus the man, love of the naked man Jesus on His cross, in His bier, the lovely child Jesus with His tiny fat penis playing on His mother's trembling knees. Life had stood still and my husband, every Saturday afternoon, had his accountants receive the workers in the town, the trades-men and the artisans with their brown felt hats and striped collarless shirts and waistcoats, as well as the poorer street hawkers, candle sellers, candy sellers, broom sellers, and a few women wrapped in shawls who hid their faces, and ever-longer lines of field hands who were not attached to any hacienda and who all owed my husband money: a long line of men and women winding down a flat, dusty, hot Saturday street of low, shuttered houses, houses chained in on themselves, the padlocks girdling every big porte cochere like chastity belts, señorita, houses jailed in on themselves, the low-slung grillwork balconies like cages on the faces of the houses—like dogs' muzzles, señorita, amiga, friend, may I call you that?

I sometimes saw them and tried to meet their eyes as I walked out to go to confession on Saturday afternoons, but one day I crossed sights with an impressive man. He was a humble peon dressed in white and with a sombrero held between powerful hands, but his face, I realized, was new; there was nothing humble about it: there was a fearful pride in it, he looked at me and held my eyes and told me right then with his gaze what I probably wanted to hear (La Luna went on: "I am poor and chained by debt. You are rich and chained by a lack of love. Let me love you one night"); such was the longing, proud fierceness of his eyes, the humorous, challenging grimace of his smiling white teeth, the rakishness of his big black mustache, the tousled, sleepless arrogance of his head. I could not help myself, señorita. Everything I had been taught told me not to do it. I should have bowed my head and gone on to church, telling the beads between my crossed hands. Instead, I stopped.

"What is your name?" was what I managed to ask that man whose head seemed too large for his short, powerful body.

The shutters of all the houses were suddenly open. The faces of all the houses were suddenly visible in the shadows of those interiors.

[153]

"Doroteo," he answered, "Doroteo Arango."

I nodded and walked on. I reached the church. I knelt in the confessional, modestly, like a woman, shielded by the grill partitions from the priest's hands, though not from his breath. I confessed my usual list of venial sins. He shook his head. "You are forgetting something."

"What, Padre?"

"You have stopped to talk to strange men on the street. Peons. Men who owe your husband money. What does this mean, my daughter? I am frightened for you!"

When I came back to my house, the line of people was gone, the shutters were closed.

Next day, in church, my confessor gave a sermon on charity. He quoted St. John on Christ chasing the money-lenders from the Temple. Yet he assured us that Christ's holy fury was in defense of the Temple, not a lack of charity toward the merchants. These He had forgiven, for His voice was that of eternal charity for all.

That night at dinner I told my husband and his family, who always gathered with us, that I had thought about what the priest had said at Mass and wondered if charity did not also mean forgiving debts.

The word fell like a cracking sheet of ice on the table.

Debts, I repeated. Forgive the debts. Not only the sins.

I was ordered from the table without supper: I was always a little girl, you see, señorita, amiga, may I call you my friend?

When he came up to my room, I was not frightened, because I knew what to say.

I love you in my own fashion. Listen to me, I told him, for your own sake.

You are indecent, he interrupted me, you say indecent

things at the table, you do indecent things in the street, you stop to talk to unknown men, low men, how dare you, you ridiculous little whore?

I looked straight at him, like the man named Doroteo looked at me, and I told him: You should be afraid. You should have looked at that man's eyes the way I did. You should be afraid. These men are different. They've taken all they can take. Now they will look at you straight in the eye and then take your life. Watch out.

He struck me and told me he would send me into the cellar if I misbehaved again.

What was there in the cellar?

I had never been there.

But the next night, on Monday, the growls started coming at all hours from under the belly of the house, as if simply by mentioning that cellar where he threatened to send me as a punishment, he had peopled it with terrors, sounds, ghosts, beasts, humming voices, instruments—I pricked up my ears, I tried to distinguish the origins of sound, the birth of a harmony that perhaps reached my ears filtered through a thousand layers of brick and wood, adobe and wallpaper, nails and mortar, yes, and even more: the veils of all that we were in that house, I, my husband, the family, the men and women waiting outside on Saturday afternoons, their own silent rumblings and divinations: will I be lent some money, will I have to repay my debt, will there be grace, will there be grace, will there be grace?

Tell me, señorita, my friend (may I?), how was I to distinguish the real source of the sounds through so many layers of being and not being and rancor and hopelessness and fear of forgetting my childhood and fear of having nothing but my childhood, fear of never being a real woman, fear of dying, as I said, withered and humbled, spoilt to no avail, like a pear left to rot in a graveyard?

Were the rumblings from the cellar those of a piano softly playing my favorite waltz, *Sobre las olas*, over and over again?

No, shrieked my husband when the rumblings from the belly of the house were stifled by the rumblings from the streets, they are the screams of the prisoners, we are going to kill all the bastards who have risen up in arms, every single one of the dirty rats, but first I am going to bring them here to my cellar to skin them alive, rats, that is what they are, what they have always been, he said, his teacup rattling against the saucer; well, it won't be only a manner of speaking now, they're going to be skinned—he stamped the cedar floor with his tiny buttoned boots wrapped in fawn-colored spats—they shall be flayed, literally peeled like overripe bananas, like worm-infested apples, like rotting pears in a graveyard. Ha! he exclaimed, and the teacup fell on his spats and stained them—if they won't line up each Saturday and pay their debts, they will line up every day of the week and be whipped to death; and those are the voices you'll hear from the cellar, my dear, he said as he bent over to wipe his spats: *Now you know.*

"But before?" I dared ask. "Before this, what were the rumblings down there?"

"How dare you question me!" he shouted, and got up, threatening me, and at that very instant, I swear to you, *mi amiga*, my friend, the bells started pealing for no reason at all, no matins, no vespers, no hour that I had known in time, and an explosion tore open our porte cochere and the men in the stained Stetsons and the barrel chests crossed with cartridge belts came in, crushing the fragile shell of the teacup, and one of them pointed out my husband—"That's him, that's the bloodsucker!" —and the man I had seen in line that Saturday long ago, the man with the fearful pride in his eyes, the man who had told me without words: "I am poor and chained by debt. You are rich and chained by a lack of love. Let me love you one night"—that man was now in my sitting room.

I knew him.

I had seen his face over and over again, in wanted posters stuck with pins to the notice board of the church, along with invitations to novenas for the souls in purgatory or reminders of the feast of St. Anthony: he was Doroteo Arango, the posters said, a cattle thief, and now he was in my parlor and he was not even looking at me but saying violently: "Take the bloodsucker back to the corral and shoot him quick. We don't have time. The Federales are hard on our heels."

Then the bells stopped ringing and the rifles cracked in the corral, ripping the afternoon as if it had been linen, and I was left alone in my parlor and swooned.

When I came to—my friend, Señorita Winslow, may I . . . ?—no one was there. A terrible silence was all around me. They had left, and I did not want to go to the corral in back of the house and see what I knew was there.

Then the Federales came in and asked what had happened. I was numb. I didn't know. Maybe my husband had been killed. Doroteo Arango . . .

"Pancho Villa," they said, correcting me. I did not understand that name then.

"They are gone now," I said simply.

"We are beating them, don't worry," they said.

"I am not worried."

"You're sure they all left?"

I nodded.

But that night, still refusing to go out to the corral and see what had to be there, I heard the rumblings from the cellar, but now they were different. I mean, the old noises were there, but now there was something more, a new humming that only I could hear, the music of a different breathing from the disconcerting panting my husband had offered up to my fear (his supreme gift to the fear he gave me in the name of marriage, as the equivalent of marriage: marriage was fear, this I had to learn and accept from him, or there was no reality to our bond, you see): I did not go out and bury him. I didn't know how many bodies there were lying around, the revolutionary dead—not victims, I refuse to call them that, just the dead, for when will we know, señorita, *mi amiga*, who was just and who was unjust? Not me. Not then. Not yet. And that new sound brought me a new fear: perhaps in the cellar of our house (I called it ours only now that my husband was surely dead) there was now something better, a treasure, yes (my childlike illusions, Señorita Harriet, coming to an end), but I knew I must keep it from following the path to death that had become my husband's.

I did not know what to do the first night after all this happened.

I dreamed that my husband was not dead, only hiding among the chickens in the netted coop, and came back to me that night, opening the doors of the bedroom with his thrusting ugly penis as I shrieked in terror: he was alive, but he was caked in blood.

[158]

I then dreamed that whatever was hidden in the cellar would be taken from me by the Federales when they came back.

This, for some obscure reason, I could not bear.

Very early next morning, I went out to the corral.

I did not look down, but I heard the buzzing flies.

I tore the boards off the coop, piled them up, carried or pushed or dragged them as best I could to the top of the cellar stairs.

The unaccustomed labor tore my long black dress, my hands that had only baked cakes and fingered the rosary and touched the lonely nipple.

I was on my knees for something other than praying for the first time in my life.

I was sweating and soaked in essences that gave off a smell I had never known existed in me, Miss Winslow.

I was sore and bruised and wounded as the nails were driven into the boards covering up the entrance to the cellar.

I wanted to protect what was there.

Or perhaps I did what I would have had to do if I had decided to give my husband a Christian burial.

The acts were similar, but his body was not present.

I let my weary body rest on the planks and said to myself: "You are smelling another body. You are sharing another breath. Those are not monsters waiting for you down there. The cellar does not hide the terrors your husband said."

Then what *was* down there?

I wanted to distinguish the things I came to desire during that long wake from those I came to hate. If my husband was not buried down there, then something that was his was certainly there, something stinking, putrid, gaseous, hairy, excremental, dripping and loathsome: I could smell it.

And I could smell something else, something I wanted.

Then the bells rang again and I knew the Federales had left and Villa's men had retaken the town. But maybe I was wrong and the bells that meant nothing meant something else. The world was not altering its realities just for me.

My doubts were resolved by a loud pistol shot from the cellar, followed by a second one, and then silence.

This was the second time I had heard shots inside my house, but this time I was not afraid.

I tore at the boards with my hands, I knew I had to free the man who fired the shots. I knew I had to pry open the cellar doors and see the dogs lying dead there first: only dogs, nothing more.

And see him come out with his lips clean.

"They were only dogs." Those were his first words to me, señorita, *mi amiga*, may I call you friend now? Do you understand, Miss Winslow?

19 Then Harriet Winslow saw General Tomás Arroyo returning to his railroad car, his head unnaturally bowed as if examining the dusty toes of his boots, seeming not to notice as the old man released Harriet and said: "Once I wrote something very funny. 'Events have been matching themselves since the beginning of Time so that I may die here.' "

His hard eyes glistened as he spoke. He murmured that

he had come here to be killed because he wasn't capable of killing himself. He had felt freed the moment he crossed the border at Juárez, as if he had walked into a different world. Now he was sure: each of us has a secret frontier within him, and that is the most difficult frontier to cross because each of us hopes to find himself alone there, but finds only that he is more than ever in the company of others.

He hesitated for an instant and then added: "This is unexpected. It's terrifying. It's painful. And it's good."

He rubbed his clean-shaven cheek with a gesture of manly resignation and, before leaving Harriet, asked: "How do I look tonight?"

She didn't answer with words; her nod told him that he was a good-looking old man.

Arroyo had told his men: "Respect the gringo. This is between him and me."

All Harriet remembered was the old gringo entering General Arroyo's private car, and that he had written about a fragmented consciousness, and she was trying to understand that as Arroyo, alien to the mystery of the two gringos, approached with a fragment of Harriet's consciousness within his own mind, this general who was wise and brave because he had understood nothing of the world outside his land, this ostentatious and arrogant man who played games with his people's beliefs and claimed the role of the great dispenser of the world's goods: she saw it all clearly in the desert light, both dying, the desert and the light, though not the General: the Mexican, Spanish, Arab caudillo followed by a retinue of servants, clients, companions, flatterers and mercenaries, a man who had possessed her and been witness to her sensuality, who had been present at the secret encounter between her soul and her body's responses, a man who had seen the moment when Harriet Winslow—who should have grown up wealthy in New York but had grown up in genteel poverty in Washington by grace of a pension and various absences—changed forever, and there inside the car was the other witness to her transformation, the man who had come to be killed, the old topographical engineer of the Indiana Volunteers who knew the value of papers, the papers that legitimized General Arroyo's quest: bounty and vengeance and lust and pride and mere acceptance by his peers. Harriet Winslow's fragmented consciousness leapt through the void into the mind of General Tomás Arroyo, who, like her, had no father; both were dead or unaware, or what is the same as dead, both unaware of their children, Harriet and Tomás: in the end, it's always death and unawareness, always the mute and insentient peace of nonexistence and unconsciousness.

Now Arroyo was climbing up the steps of the railroad car and she was running toward him, crying, Stop! stop! and the woman with the moon face had run from the other end of the car and was struggling to hold her when they heard the shots, accompanied by Arroyo's gargling sounds of rage but no sound at all from the old man, who managed to stagger out to the platform with the burned papers in his hand, and behind him Arroyo, still firing, in a rage like none Harriet Winslow had ever seen before or ever expected to see again; as Arroyo was witness to her sensuality, she was witness to death. Arroyo, standing with a smoking revolver in one hand and a long, flat, empty box of splintered rosewood in the other.

She had screamed at Arroyo to stop him: Think; in making love to each other they had known who they

were, they had each bid farewell to an absent father, but
also to their youth: she, consciously; he, by pure intuition;
in the name of their lost youth, she begged him not to kill
the only father either of them had known.

The first time she cried out with pleasure had been
with him; he cried out for the first time with the woman
with the moon face, after living so long in the silence
the hacienda imposed on its slaves.

The old gringo fell dead and Harriet Winslow
wanted to believe that he died wondering, as she now
wondered, whether the sun would come out tonight,
because from now on the sun would be her terror, not
the darkness (now she sits alone and remembers). The
old gringo fell dead and the earth was eternally alone
in the middle of the sea, and the desert was eternally
alone in the middle of the earth: he fell dead on the
unique ocean of the earth; the old gringo fell dead and the
words had been turned to ashes; the old gringo fell dead
and his companions would have to speak now because
the papers with their history would no longer speak for
them. They would say: We worked this land for a
thousand years before the surveyors and the lawyers and
the army came to tell us, This land is not yours, this land
has been sold, but stay here anyway, live here and serve
the new owners, for if you don't, you'll die of hunger. The
old gringo died and the words on the papers went flying
across the desert, saying, We like to fight, we feel dead
if we aren't fighting, pray God this revolution never ends,
but if it ends, we'll go fight in a new revolution, fight till
we drop into our graves. The old gringo fell dead; and the
scorched words went flying far beyond the hacienda and
the village and the church, saying, We never knew anyone
outside this region, we didn't know there was a world

beyond our maize fields, now we know people from all parts, we sing our songs together, we dream our dreams together and argue whether we were happier isolated in our villages or now, whirling around everywhere, dizzied by so many dreams and so many different songs. The old gringo fell dead and the song of the scorched words spread across the desert inhabited by the ghosts of lakes and rivers and oceans: it's all ours now because we took it, girls, clothes, money, horses; all we want is to go on like this till we die. The old gringo was dead, his back riddled with bullet holes, and the words were devoured by the alkaline wind he would never breathe again, deaf forever to the words that say, Beaten if we weren't on our feet by four in the morning to work until sundown, beaten if we spoke to each other while we worked, beaten if they heard us making love, the only times we escaped being beaten was as babies crying, or as old men dying. When he died, the old gringo fell face down in the dust, the mountains moved a step closer, and the lowering clouds sought their mirror in the earth, seeing their image in the fiery words: The worst master was the one who said he loved us like a father, insulting us with his compassion, treating us like children, like idiots, like savages; we're none of those; in our minds we know we're none of those. When the old gringo bit the dust in Mexico, rain fell upon the desert as if to settle both blood and dust, and great sheets of water soaked the earth's shroud so the scorched words would be as water, saying, Things were far away, now they're near and we don't know whether this is good or bad; now everything is so near to us we can touch it, and we're afraid: is that what the Revolution is? When the old gringo went away forever, the mountains looked like petrified sand and the sky was dying beneath a rain of words that said everything was far away but Pancho Villa is near, and he's like us, we're all Villas!

When the old gringo died, life dared not come to a halt.

Harriet Winslow and the old gringo had watched him earlier, out of earshot, haranguing, persuading, putting his arms around this man's shoulders, pinching that woman's cheek, saying they didn't need lessons or committees, what they needed were the balls for war and the love for peace, machine guns by day and kisses by night, where does a man prove himself? in battle or in bed, not in some election, he shouted above the braying of the burros with the foam-flecked muzzles: the Revolution is one big family, we all go together, the important thing is for us to go forward together, I depend on Villa as if he were my father and I depend on you as if you were my family; everything else can wait, except winning this war. He swept up a naked child and playfully spanked its buttocks, and they watched him from a distance, imagining that he was filling their ears with, I screwed the gringa woman, but that wasn't important, nothing was important but to own the land, everything else owns you, and it's bad to go through life thinking about what you own and being afraid to lose it, instead of living like a man and dying with honor and dignity.

But now the old gringo was dead and the rain was over and the desert smelled of wet creosote bush and General Tomás Arroyo was speaking to his great, silent, barefoot family: Look, look what I saved for you, the ballroom, the special places that used to be only for them. I didn't touch that, I burned all the rest, the image of your servitude, their store where our children's children would still owe the shirt off their backs, I burned that, the stables where the horses ate better than we did, the barracks where the Federal soldiers watched us all day, picking their teeth and sharpening their bayonets, you remember all that? the dining rooms where they stuffed themselves, the bedrooms filled with their fucking and their snoring, the polluted water, the stinking communal latrines, the mad dogs I see and fear in my dreams, my God, I destroyed it all for you, except for this building that, if we survive, will belong to you. A ballroom of mirrors.

"I spent my childhood spying. No one knew me. From my hiding places I knew them all. All because one day I discovered the ballroom of mirrors and I discovered I had a face and a body. I could see myself. Tomás Arroyo. For you, Rosario, Remedios, Jesús, Benjamín, José, Colonel García, Chencho Mansalvo, even you, La Garduña, in the name of the fleas and the straw sleeping mats, in the name of . . ."

Everyone was watching him now with a kind of fear, afraid for themselves and for him. Watching their leader, watching their protector, watching him with sadness. Pedrito watched him, Pedrito, who in 1914 had been a boy of eleven with a perforated silver peso in his shirt pocket, a peso he had retrieved in the church from between the feet of the faithful: look in this mirror and you will see yourselves.

"I'm no better than any of you, my children. But I am the one who safeguards the papers. Someone has to do it. The papers are the only proof we have that these lands are ours. They are the testament of our ancestors. Without the papers, we're like orphans. I fight, you fight, every one of us fights so that these papers will be respected. Our lives . . . our souls . . ."

"I will never understand you," Harriet had said.

And now the rain was over and the old gringo he'd asked them to respect was lying dead beneath a rainbow spilling across the dusk. The desert mirrored itself; it gnawed at the bottom of the ancient sea, the coarse sand of the great beach the waters had left behind, and General Tomás Arroyo, who because he had the papers had never spoken much, now had to speak in the name of the burned papers. Now memory depended on their leader, but it also depended on them. But the woman with the moon face knew that Tomás Arroyo was not a man of words but the man who kept the words.

Which is why she said, very quietly, to the trembling American: "When he talks so much, something is going to happen to him. Silence is his best friend."

It was the troops themselves that quickly brought an end to their leader's words, surging forward on the tide of their own voices, urging him to action, telling him he was right, they would live in spite of him. "It's time for us to move on. It's time to leave the mirrors behind, General. Things'll go bad for us if we don't join up with Villa. We may be a floating brigade, but we won't get to Mexico City on our own."

"My destiny is my own," said Arroyo, when he was alone.

"What will the gringa do to him?" the woman with the moon face asked La Garduña at the hour when one whispers in secret, not to awaken the earth: What will she do to my man?

But La Garduña just cackled and said in a loud voice,

not worrying about the world's repose, that the papers and the mirrors didn't matter a Wilson to her, as everyone said in Villa's troops.

"What does matter to you?" asked the woman with the moon face.

And La Garduña remembered that she'd been lonely and innocent in her village in Durango, protected by the saintliness of her Aunt Josefa Arreola, when the first revolutionary troops had passed through and she'd gone out into the street, excited, and seen a handsome boy, but a boy with death written in his eyes, who'd caught her eye, who'd moved and seemed to call to her, so he wouldn't be alone. She'd felt a kind of sad but pleasant warmth, something like pity, and she'd never gone back home but stayed by the side of the boy, who was a father to her daughter until a bullet killed him in the battle of La Ascensión. That's how she became a whore, they said.

"At least, my destiny is my own," General Tomás Arroyo said to himself many times in his uneasy dreams the night he killed the old gringo and it rained in the desert and the burned words went screaming on the wind.

 Pancho Villa rode into Camargo one brilliant spring morning: his copper-hard head was crowned by a large gold-embroidered sombrero, a sombrero stained with dust and blood, not a luxury but an instrument of power and a symbol of struggle, like his wide, callused hands and his bronze stirrups buffed by the mountain winds. A patina of gunpowder, thorn, and rock, pine trails and endless, blinding plains clung to his rough antelope-colored suit, his chamois leggings, his steel machete and silver parade goad, the gold and silver buttons of his short jacket and trousers, everything gleaming with silver and gold, not precious treasures to be hoarded but metals to adorn us in battle and in death: a suit of lights.

Villa was a man of the north, tall and robust, his torso longer than his short Indian legs, but with long arms and powerful hands and a head that might have been lopped long ago from the body of another man, in former times and distant places, a severed head from the past welded like a precious metal casque to a mortal body, powerful but powerless, from the present. Oriental eyes, smiling but cruel, set in a plain of laugh lines; a ready smile, teeth shining like kernels of white corn; a scrawny mustache and three days' growth of beard; a head that had been seen in Mongolia and Andalusia and the Rif, among the nomadic tribes of North America, and was now here in Camargo, Chihuahua, grinning and blinking and squinting against the onslaught of the light, a head stored with vast reserves of intuition and ferocity and generosity, a head come to rest on the shoulders of Pancho Villa.

The landowners had fled and the moneylenders were

in hiding. A laughing Villa scarcely reined in his chest-
nut horse on the rocky streets of Camargo, where the
central column of the Northern Division had come to
join those of the other generals before attacking Zacatecas, the commercial center of the ruined haciendas he
had sacked to free people from slavery and usury and
debt. Villa's horse's hoofs clattered on the cobbles, pre-
ceding a train of metallic sounds that rang in counter-
point to the strange hollowness of the stone streets:
copper and steel bits and curbs and curb chains jingled
and clinked; horsehair crops and quirts hissed and whips
cracked in the air.

All the town was out, throwing confetti from wrought-
iron balconies, draping serpentines from lampposts,
muffling the encounter between metal and stone in a
tide of the pink, blue, and scarlet of Mexican fiestas,
overflowing large glass demijohns of refreshing drinks,
many-colored candy slices, and huge earthen casseroles
bubbling with black and red and green sauces.

The reporters were there, too, the gringo newspapermen and photographers, with a new invention, the movie
camera. Villa was already captivated, he didn't have to
be convinced a second time. He was well aware that the
little machine could capture the ghost of his body if not
the flesh of his soul—that belonged only to him, to his
dear dead mother, and to the Revolution; his moving
body, generous and domineering, his panther-like body,
that, yes, could be captured and set free again in a dark-
room, like a Lazarus risen not from the dead but from
faraway times and spaces, in a black room on a white
wall, anywhere, in New York or in Paris. He promised
Walsh, the gringo with the camera: "Don't worry, don
Raúl. If you say the light at four in the morning isn't

right for your little machine, well, no problem. The executions will take place at six. But no later. Afterwards we march and fight. Understood?"

Now all the Yankee newspapermen gathered in Camargo were besieging him with questions before he moved on Zacatecas to decide the fate of the revolution against Huerta and, in passing, the fate of Wilson's Mexican policy. "Do you expect the United States government to recognize you if you win?"

"That problem doesn't exist. I am subordinate to Carranza, the first leader of the Revolution."

"Everyone knows that you and Carranza don't get along, General."

"Who knows it? Do you know it? Tell me about it, please."

"We intercepted a telegram your General Maclovio Herrera sent to Carranza after you were denied the right to launch your attack on Zacatecas, General Villa. The text is very brief. It says, 'You son of a bitch.'"

"Oh, my little friend. I don't know how to say those bad words in Spanish. I swear to you, I can only say them in English. In any case, Señor Carranza has decided to send the Arrieta brothers to take Zacatecas."

"But you're here with a whole division, with artillery and ten thousand men . . ."

"At the service of the Revolution, señores. If the Arrieta brothers, as they usually do, get stuck in Zacatecas, I can be there in five days' time to give them a hand. That's all I need!"

"And last, General Villa. What do you think of the American occupation of Veracruz?"

"An unwelcome guest and a dead man both stink after two days."

"Can you be a little more specific, General?"

"The Marines landed in Veracruz after bombarding the city and killing young Mexican cadets. Instead of swamping Huerta, they made him stronger by rousing the people's patriotism. They split support for the Revolution and made it possible for Huerta, that drunken bum, to impose his filthy levy. Boys who thought they were being sent to fight the gringos in Veracruz were sent to fight against me in Coahuila. I don't know whether that's what you're looking for, but it seems to me that when gringos aren't too smart for their own good, they're plenty dumb."

"Is it true you had an American officer shot in the back? That a captain in the United States Army was killed in cold blood by one of your own men, General?"

"What the shit . . . ?"

"Responsible sources in the United States have branded you as nothing less than a common bandit, General Villa. Public opinion questions whether you can guarantee safety here in Mexico. Do you respect human life? Can you deal with civilized nations?"

"Who the shit said all this?"

"A Miss . . . uh, Harriet Winslow . . . uh, from Washington, D.C. She says she was witness to the events. Her father had been missing in action ever since the war in Cuba. It seems he had only wanted to avoid family obligations, but decided he wanted to see his little girl, a grown woman now, before he died. She came here to see him. They've accused a general in your army, General Villa. What did ya say his name is, Art?"

"Arroyo's the name. General Tomás Arroyo. She says she saw him shoot her daddy dead."

"With all due respect, General, we remind you that

the bodies of United States citizens killed in Mexico, or anywhere else in the world, must be returned on the request of their families, to be given a decent Christian burial."

"Is that what the law says?" Villa grunted.

"Indeed it does, General."

"Show me where it's written."

"Many of our laws are unwritten, General Villa."

"A law that isn't written down on paper? Then why the devil learn to read?" a bewildered Villa replied, with a scornful grin. Then he laughed, and they all laughed with him, and stepped aside for the man who symbolized the Revolution and who was preparing to show the world that it wasn't Carranza, a perfumed old senator, one of the so-called decent people of Mexico, who deserved that appellation but precisely what Carranza most despised, a barefoot, illiterate, pulque-swilling, taco-chomping campesino from the restless hills of Durango who had been beaten by the same hacienda owners who raped his sisters. No, he laughed, and he assured his distinguished artillery commander General Felipe Ángeles, a graduate of the French Academy of St.-Cyr, I don't say this to you, don Felipe, but to them, you've just seen them; the gringos act as if we didn't exist, and then one fine day they discover us, and watch out! we're the devil himself ready to take their lives and property; well, why not give them a real scare—Pancho Villa grinned—why not invade them for once and let them see what it feels like?

Then he flew into a terrible rage to think there might be anyone who didn't understand his situation. Carranza had him paralyzed in Chihuahua, so Villa wouldn't be the one to lead the way to Mexico City, so the glory would go to the pretty boys, oh, what griped his balls most was that that old he-goat bastard never let a chance go by to remind the former cattle rustler from Chihuahua that they came from very different backgrounds: no, being a lousy lawyer *isn't* the same as risking your hide! He asked his secretary, the professor, to write his resignation from the Division, so the fat's in the fire, let's see whether Natera and the fancy Arrieta brothers could take Zacatecas by themselves, see why that hypocrite Pablo González hadn't sent coal or munitions from Monterrey, and see whether their civil authority would do them any good without Pancho Villa's military support; let's get it decided here and now. And to think that on top of everything else, some shitass hanging around in Chihuahua is making problems for me with the gringos! Villa exploded, but, as always, was calmed by a night of lovemaking.

General Tomás Arroyo received the order to dig up the gringo wherever he was and bring him to Camargo. No, they'd lied to him on purpose. No family was claiming the body, but a newspaper, the *Washington Star*, he was told. But when this order finally tore the flying brigade away from the burned hacienda of the Mirandas, Arroyo knew full well the name of the person who was claiming the body. He saw her in his dreams, with the old man's blasted head in her arms, looking at Arroyo standing in the door of the railroad car, as if he had killed something that belonged to her, but also to him; and now they were both alone again, orphans, looking at each other with hatred, no longer capable of nourishing each other through a living creature, or of filling the tormented void that she felt in herself and he in him.

"Look what he has in his hand! Look what he has

clenched in his hand." This was all Arroyo could say. She saw the burned papers and Arroyo was saying that the gringo had burned his soul, and she admitted he had burned something more: the history of Mexico; but that was no excuse, because the life of a person is worth more than the history of a country, and Harriet Winslow was convinced that, in spite of everything, the desert of Chihuahua cried out with her: murderer, pig, greaser, stinking coward! She screamed at him: You had me, but you had to kill him, too.

"He came here to provoke me," Arroyo said, panting. "Just like you. You both came to provoke me. Fucking, sonofabitching gringos!"

No, you provoked yourself, she said, as that long day came to an end, you provoked yourself to prove to yourself who you are. Your name isn't Arroyo, like your mother's; your name is Miranda, after your father. Yes, she said, as the rain dissolved the ashes of the papers, you're the resentful heir, disguised as a rebel.

"You poor bastard. You are Tomás Miranda."

She said it savagely, wanting to wound him, but knowing she could have said it calmly to the old man lying beside the wheels of the railroad car, every bullet hole clearly visible on his back; but she said it with rage for the sake of justice, to remind him that she, too, could fight, fight back, blow for blow. Tomás was beyond understanding anything. He had killed the old gringo. He couldn't imagine that Harriet Winslow still had fight left in her; she must feel as drained as he. The old gringo, and the burned papers.

"I would have taken anything from you two gringos. Anything, except this," Arroyo said, pointing to the ruin of the papers.

"You needn't worry," Harriet Winslow replied, with her few remaining remnants of humor and compassion. "He thought he was already dead."

But on that evening Arroyo wanted to burn his own soul. "What is the life of an old man compared to the rights of my people?"

"I just told you, you killed a dead man. Be thankful. You saved yourself the expense of an execution."

An execution was what Villa demanded of Tomás Arroyo when he saw the old man's bullet-riddled body, as he checked the famous temper that terrorized both his own men and his enemies. Pancho Villa touched the bullet-riddled back of the old gringo and remembered something one of the Yankee reporters had told him when they interviewed him in Camargo: "I have a saying for you, General Villa. 'What we call dying is simply the last pain.'"

"Who said that?"

"Oh, a bitter old man."

"Then it was written?"

"As I said, by a bitter old man."

"Oh, by . . ."

Villa ordered the execution for that same night, for midnight. He warned it would be a secret execution; no one was to know anything about it except him, Villa, General Arroyo, and the firing squad. Let Mr. Walsh and his camera go fuck themselves. This wasn't for him.

With some difficulty, they propped the old gringo against the wall, facing the firing squad, his head drooping on his chest, his knees limp, his face slightly disfigured by the acids of his first burial in the desert.

The order was given in the patio behind Villa's head-

[176]

quarters; the light of the lanterns placed at intervals on the ground cast strange shadows on the men's faces. Shots rang out and the old gringo fell for the second time into the arms of his old friend, death.

"Now he is legally shot from the front, in accordance with the law," said Pancho Villa.

"What do we do with the corpse, General?" asked the commander of the firing squad.

"We're going to send it to whoever claimed it in the United States. We'll say he died in a battle against the Federales, that they captured him and shot him."

Villa didn't look at Arroyo but said he didn't want to be dragging around the body of any gringo that could give Wilson an excuse to recognize Carranza or intervene against Villa in the north.

"We'll kill a few gringos, all right," said Villa with a ferocious grin, "but in good time and when I decide."

He turned to Arroyo without changing expression. "He was a brave man, wasn't he? A brave gringo? I've heard about all he did. Now he's been shot fairly, from the front, not in the back like a coward, because he wasn't a coward, was he, Tomás Arroyo?"

"No, General. The gringo was the bravest of us all."

"Here, Tomasito. Give him the coup de grâce. You know you're like a son to me. Do it well. We have to do everything aboveboard and according to the law. This time I don't want you to make me any mistakes. We have to be ready for anything. It seems to me you had a good rest at that hacienda, you were there long enough and even became famous, right?"

("Arroyo," said the Yankee newspaperman. "Arroyo is the name.")

"Yes, General," Arroyo answered simply.

Arroyo walked to where the body of the old gringo lay before the wall, knelt beside him, and pulled out his Colt. He administered the coup de grâce with precision. No blood flowed from the old gringo's neck now. Then Villa gave the order to fire on the unfortunate Arroyo, whose face was the living image of pain and disbelief. Even so, he managed to call out, "Viva Villa!"

Arroyo fell beside the old gringo, and Villa said he wouldn't put up with officers playing their little games with foreigners and creating unnecessary problems for him. When it came to killing gringos, only he, Pancho Villa, would say when and why. The body of the old man would be sent back with his daughter and the matter would be forgotten forever.

The eyes, the blazing blue eyes of the old Indiana General, were closed forever that night in Camargo by the hands of a boy with eyes black as marbles and with two bandoliers slung across his chest, a boy who one day had asked, "You want to meet Pancho Villa?"

Pedrito pulled from his pants pocket the peso perforated by the same Colt .44 that Arroyo had thrown to the old gringo, and placed it in the stained shirt pocket of the man who had died twice. Villa himself administered the coup de grâce to Tomás Arroyo.

21 Harriet Winslow identified the bullet-riddled body of the old man but she said yes, this is my father, and she buried him in Arlington Cemetery beside her mother, who had died near her lamp on the old lamp table, conquered finally by the shadows. So that first Harriet had thought of her poor mother, who had so wanted her to be a cultivated and respected young lady —although chivalry was little in evidence to a family in strained circumstances. The refinement of the spirit demands a social complement in everyday life: the presence of a gentleman. She had made allowances for both prejudices and differences of opinion, and trusted that in the end happiness would prevail and order triumph. Harriet Winslow thought how someday she herself would rest here beside her mother and a lonely old writer who had gone to Mexico to be killed.

"The old gringo came here to die."

The night of his death, she had wandered dazed through the camp; suddenly she felt an overwhelming hunger she knew was not physical in origin but that only food could appease. On a whim, she sat down by a woman cooking tortillas over a small, smoking brazier. Mutely, she asked whether she could help. She took a small portion of the cornmeal mixture and formed tortillas, imitating the woman squatting beside her. Then she tasted them.

"You like tortillas?" the woman asked.

"I do."

"They're good. Soon we'll be leaving. We've been here a long time now."

"I know. This is his place. He really doesn't want to leave."

[179]

"Ah, well, it can't be helped. We have to keep going. I follow my man, I cook for him and bear his children. Life doesn't stop just because of a war. Will you be going with him?"

"Whom do you mean?"

"With our General Arroyo. Aren't you his new woman?"

While she sat eating her tortilla beside the woman that long-ago night in the desert; or later, while she was sitting beside the old man's tomb inscribed with her father's name; or still later, as an old woman, alone, remembering all those things, she prepared herself for a sense of compassion she had betrayed perhaps only once in her life, when she demanded the old gringo's body, knowing what the consequences would be. The new compassion granted her precisely by virtue of that sin, she owed to a young Mexican revolutionary who offered life and to an old American writer who sought death: they had given her enough life to live for many years, here in the United States, there in Mexico, anywhere at all: pity was the name of the emotion Harriet Winslow had felt when she looked into the face of violence and glory, and both were finally unmasked to show their true features: those of death.

Then came the Great War, and the Revolution on the southern frontier was swept off the front pages of the newspapers until Villa attacked a border town in New Mexico, and General Pershing was sent to chase him through the mountains of Chihuahua and of course never found him, not only because Villa knew those barrancas and dusty roads blindfolded, but for another, more powerful reason: Pancho Villa could be killed only by the traitor within.

That, thinks Harriet Winslow, is why, in spite of everything, she wished she had been present at the execution of General Tomás Arroyo, to see with her own eyes the flight of that destiny he always thought was his own, rooted in his will, not that of another person. But he died at the hands of his leader Pancho Villa and that ended any destiny at all. She always asked herself what Tomás Arroyo might have done had he survived (the Revolution killed him), what his destiny would have been in the future of Mexico. As the old gringo died, he may have burned a dual future: Tomás Arroyo's and Mexico's.

After the deaths, Harriet Winslow left her Camargo hotel room. At midnight she had heard the fusillade in the distance: the old gringo had died for the second time. Then there was a second round of shots—a first death—followed by a single shot. Arroyo also died twice.

At the reception desk of the hotel—a tiled patio with potted plants and canaries—the woman with the moon face was waiting for her.

She didn't speak. Harriet followed her to a ruined chapel. Pancho Villa was standing in the doorway and said to them: Go in and see your men.

There lay the bodies of Tomás Arroyo and the old gringo. The woman with the moon face began to weep, and then to cry out, but Harriet Winslow remembered that Tomás Arroyo had cried out for the first time with this inconsolable woman, from the pure pleasure of being able to cry out when making love to a woman; and Harriet Winslow remembered that in the same way she had first cried out in pleasure with this dead man.

"My macho, my son, my man," keened Tomás Arroyo's woman on the night of his wake in a church in Camargo, where a Christ caged in glass, crowned with thorns and covered with a mantle of mockery, stared at them from His stand on an empty beer case.

All Harriet Winslow said to the old gringo's corpse was: "An empty grave is waiting for you in a military cemetery, Papa."

They also left Camargo together the following morning, biting and chill: two wooden coffins on two carts pulled by two tired mules. La Garduña, Inocencio Mansalvo, and young Pedro accompanied them as far as the crossroads. No one spoke. La Garduña was carrying her little girl wrapped in her rebozo, and when they came to the crossing, she again thanked Harriet Winslow. "You'll see, my daughter will see to it that I'm buried in holy ground beside my Aunt Josefa Arreola in Durango."

"I hope you will live many years," said Harriet Winslow.

"Who knows? But I will die thinking of my little unborn brother, the angel, and giving thanks to you . . ."

"Where, doña, will they bury General Arroyo?" Inocencio Mansalvo asked the woman with the moon face.

She answered, with dry eyes, that she was going to bury him in the desert, where nothing more would ever be heard of him.

"I wish I could go with you," said Inocencio. "But I must escort the American woman. General Villa's orders."

Tomás Arroyo's woman nodded, prodded the old mule, and set off toward her unknown destination just as Colonel Frutos García was arriving to pay his last respects to his leader. The cart slowly disappeared into a cloud of dust and Frutos García looked at Harriet and said that they would escort her as far as the border, Inocencio

Mansalvo and young Pedrito, too; he was a brave boy and he'd loved the old gringo very much. Besides, he added with a dash of Spanish roguishness, with a boy along, no one would get any ideas.

"You must not worry," he added, more seriously now. "You did what you had to do. The old gringo came to die in Mexico. My God, who could have told him he was going to die over a gringa? In truth, he died because he crossed the frontier. Wasn't that reason enough?"

"I did, too. I crossed it," said Harriet.

"Don't worry. We will respect both you and the old gringo. The old gringo, because he was brave. Because he had sorrow in his eyes. And because that was the last order our General Tomás Arroyo gave: Respect the old gringo."

"And me?"

"You, because you are the one who will remember it all."

Then he said goodbye and rode away.

On the long road from Camargo to Ciudad Juárez, Harriet Winslow had a long time to think about her life after she returned to Washington. But she felt a warm presence beside her now: a Mexican boy. Pedrito had loved the dead man who was being taken to the grave of Captain Winslow in Arlington. Inocencio Mansalvo took charge of everything on their journey: food and shelter, route and safety. He knew these unmarked roads very well. This territory was already in the camp of the Revolution, and here everyone was a Villista.

In Juárez, as Harriet was preparing to cross to the other side, young Pedrito spoke for the first time. "It happened the way you wanted, old man," he said in farewell to the gringo's corpse, while Harriet shuffled through the bureaucratic papers needed for the difficult entry of a dead body into the United States of America. "The way you wanted it, old man. Pancho Villa himself gave you the coup de grâce."

Inocencio Mansalvo leaned, smoking, on the railing of the bridge. Burning in the heat of the border spring, he beckoned brusquely to Harriet. She obeyed his summons. This was her farewell to Mexico. Unspeaking, the two stared for a while at the swift but shallow dark waters of the river North Americans call the Grande and Mexicans call the Bravo.

For the first time Harriet really looked at Mansalvo. He was a thin man, with green eyes and hair black as an Oriental's; two deep clefts furrowed his cheeks, two marked the corners of his mouth, and two crossed his forehead, all in pairs, as if twin artisans had hurriedly hacked him out with a machete, the sooner to thrust him out in the world. Even his handsome chin was split. Harriet chewed on her lip; until today, until this minute, she had never *looked* at this man.

She stared at him standing motionless and inscrutable, cleft in two from chin up, and she knew that he would always keep his eye on the long northern border of Mexico, because for Mexicans the only reason for war was always the gringos.

In spite of himself, Mansalvo looked across at the North American side of the border. "The old gringo used to say there weren't any more frontiers for the gringos, not to the east or the west, not to the north, only to the south, always to the south," said the guerrilla, unfolding a newspaper clipping.

Harriet, leaning on the railing beside Mansalvo, could smell the man's alcohol, onion and black tobacco sweat.

With him, she looked at the face of the old gringo in the clipping from a North American newspaper. Inocencio Mansalvo dropped the clipping into the river.

"What a shame," he said. "I can't read English. Now you won't be able to read me what it said."

Then Mansalvo turned and forcefully grasped Harriet by the arms. "What a shame! Why didn't you fall in love with me? My general would still be alive today." He let her go.

"Always to the south," Inocencio Mansalvo repeated. "What a shame. They're right when they say this isn't a border. It's a scar."

Then he walked away and Harriet watched Inocencio Mansalvo's receding back, the chamois jacket over a collarless shirt, the dirt-covered Stetson spraying dirt to the rhythm of his Mexican *vaquero*'s stride.

Harriet didn't look at them again, not at him, not at the boy. When she crossed over to El Paso, a swarm of newspapermen were waiting for her. They, rather than the customs officials, had ascertained that Captain Winslow, missing in action in Cuba, surely confused, a victim of amnesia and of mistreatment in the Spanish prison camps, but infused with the martial courage his admirable daughter had recognized and rescued from the bloody battles of the Mexican revolutionaries . . . Harriet listened and assimilated the story spun by the press, accepting it as a fragment of the time she was to safeguard. The casket was placed on an army limber to be transported to the railroad station.

"You're national news, Miss Winslow. Your friend in Washington, a Mr. Delaney, has stated that the Senate will be honored to hear you testify on the current barbarism in Mexico."

Harriet stood still. Seeing him move away, she was afraid she would lose contact with her companion, the "recovered" corpse, a roving consciousness lost in death, more than ever in death, a consciousness peopled by ghosts, murdered fathers and lost sons.

"Miss Winslow . . . national news . . ."

A blue haze once more separated her from the old man: Harriet reached out a hand as if to hold back the errant corpse from the manmade haze, a steaming fog of punctuality and energy; to prevent their being separated, they, the two gringos who had come to Mexico, he consciously, she unintentionally, to confront the next frontier of American consciousness, the most difficult of all, Harriet nearly shouted, national news, national news, trying to detach herself from the group of newspapermen so she would not be separated from the corpse of the old man, the most difficult frontier of all, the strangest, because it was the closest and therefore the one most often forgotten, most often ignored, and most feared when it stirred from its long lethargy.

("What a shame. Why didn't you fall in love with me?")

"Fiske, *San Francisco Chronicle*. You haven't answered my question. Will you testify, so we can bring progress and democracy to Mexico? Realize . . ."

"*We* bring? Who?" asked Harriet, turning in circles, bewildered, separated from her dead man, her companion, seeing on one side a sunstruck suspension bridge and moribund dust; on the other, the quicksilver path of the rails and the blue haze of the railroad station: the casket wrapped in the United States flag.

"Who! The United States, Miss Winslow. You are an American citizen."

"Fiske's the name. You called me and stated that your father had been brutally murdered."

"National news . . ."

"We were proud to help you. Now you . . ."

"Do you think we should intervene in Mexico?"

"Don't you want to avenge your father's death?"

"*San Francisco Chronicle* . . ."

"*Washington Star* . . ."

"Don't you want us to save Mexico for democracy and progress, Miss Winslow?"

"No! No! I want to learn to live with Mexico, I don't want to save it," she blurted out, and fled from the group of newspapermen, fled from the corpse of the old man, ran back toward the border, the river, the weary sun of that day dying over the western border, ran as if she had forgotten something she did not tell the newspapermen, as if she wanted to tell something to those she had left behind, as if she could make them understand that those words meant nothing, "save Mexico for progress and democracy," that what mattered was to live with Mexico in spite of progress and democracy, that each of us carries his Mexico and his United States within him, a dark and bloody frontier we dare to cross only at night: that's what the old gringo had said.

She looked at young Pedrito and Inocencio Mansalvo on the other side of the river. She called to them, asking them to forgive her for the death of Tomás Arroyo, but they didn't hear her, and if they had, they wouldn't have understood her. *I only carried out Arroyo's wishes to die young, to take his time, safeguard it for him.*

They didn't hear her call as the bridge burst into flames: "I have been here. This land will always be a part of me."

[187]

Their backs were turned to her, and they saw her forever entering a mirror-lined ballroom without looking at herself, because, in reality, she was entering a dream.

I looked into that house, Arroyo said later (later, she now sits alone and remembers), and I saw my mother married. My mother married in my father's house. I saw my father's wife and saw her as a spinster. I willed her so. No one had touched my father's legitimate wife. He had not touched her. He had touched my mother; I was born. My mother was married to him, not his lawfully wedded wife. She was not what I had imagined with old Graciano that evening which marked me forever, gringuita. She was yellow as an old, cracked cheese, curled up from being left uneaten for too long. She was black as her clothes, the blackness of the clothes imitating the blackness of all the recesses of her hidden flesh. Mortified, mortified: what we hear since childhood in church, the mortification of the flesh, the confession of all sins, the pardon of all sins before we die—is your church as harsh and as kind as ours, gringa, as quick to attribute sin but also as quick to absolve it? When my father's legal wife came to the chapel on feast days, I wondered if she would be absolved after confessing her sins; for I could not imagine my father kneeling and saying "Forgive me": that was she, the bearer of my father's sins since she was the happy recipient of his wealth, his name, his care; she must have to pay for all this by confessing for him. I could never see him kneeling. Instead, he had offered my mother no joy, no wealth, but no sin either: I was not a sin, I her only possession was not, I repeat, a sin. I had nothing to confess, ever. Not even my transforming of the legitimate wife into a withered, black, untouched woman. And he? My most secret desire was to be with him after he died. Not when he died; don Graciano deserved that more than my father ever did, and I had not given him that. No. I swore that if by some strange fate I came to be present at my father's death, I would refuse him my eyes, even if he begged for them to lead him on the road to death. I swore that I would reserve my eyes for his corruption, I would disinter him and take him with me and stay with him for all the days and nights that were needed so as to see his flesh decay, his hair grow and then stop, his creeping nails scratch the stillness of the world, and then stop, too; his eyelids crumble and the look of death reappear, defying me to gaze on it, his bones appear as white and clean as the heads of dead calves in the desert. How long, do you know, does it take for this real death, the absolute nakedness of bone (she asked him before he could ask her)? How long for the sheer essence of our eternity on earth to appear, Arroyo, how long, above all, for us to tolerate the sight not only of what we shall be but of eternity on earth as it truly is, without fairy tales, without faith in the spirit or acceptance of the resurrection? How long would you have stayed watching your father, Arroyo? How long would you have watched death after death, Arroyo, without knowing, you poor brave fool, that death is only what happens inside us—all right, you are right, but not the way you think, not death inseparable from life as you think, but death instead of life while we think we are living? I, Harriet Winslow, was in so many ways living a death inside of me, knowing that I was dead and that because I knew it death could only occur inside me, only inside of me, and the rest did not count. Now you tell me, General Tomás Arroyo, you tell me if I have come out of myself, somehow, mysteriously, I myself know not how, and having lived my death inside me only, have now come out to the life outside me, the life I ignored, I admit it now; and you are part of that life, but only a part, my little man, do not be proud of yourself, there are a million things rushing forth, and my words, my dreams, my time, even if doubled as you said of the old man, who would hate us if we gave him the gift, as you say, of another seventy years to live, would detest us for it: oh, is he doomed by others rather than you, Arroyo? He is part of the life outside me which now miraculously seems to be the only life inside me, do you understand? And so is your lover the Luna woman, and so is the poor woman whose daughter's life I saved even as I doubted if it was worth saving, if I could ever have a child and then save its own life as I saved the life of an unknown, unnamed. Arroyo, I know, I have not looked at all of your people, I wish I had, I have certainly missed something, what have I missed? Is there a pair of eyes that should have met mine, am I derelict in establishing, for the first time, a world outside myself, outside my own closed world, am I, Arroyo? You must tell me. *I cannot take it all in in such a short time.* I am weak and foreign and, even in my shabby gentility, sheltered. Do you understand this? Yet I have learned. I am making an effort, I swear it. I am trying to understand all this, you, your country, your people. But I am also a part of my own people, I cannot deny what I am, Arroyo, and all that I have here is not father or mother or anything else but only the old man, he is the only thing I can recognize myself in here, as I try to understand all of you. Only he, you hear? You have made me hear you all (tell me if I'm missing something, Arroyo), and I have tried to understand why you are doing all this. But if you do something that lets me see that you will do to them the things that they are fighting against, the death-within-them that they are fleeing from in this drowning movement in which we are all caught, if I think you are going to hurt them as you yourself were hurt as a boy, Arroyo, then, Arroyo, you will have killed me and sent me back into the isolation which is my own death, the only death I have known, ever. But I will not forgive you for that, Arroyo. Do not do anything against your people. But also, do not do anything against my *only* people: the old man who writes, Arroyo. I will not forgive you that, she said.

Then the bodies from the encounter on the night of the squealing pigs were laid out around the square in front of the church. Harriet had seen the reproduction of one of the Masters that her great-uncle both hated and desired, desired if they were famous and priceless, but hated when even their fame could not disguise their distortion of reality, their perspectives outrageously unreal and self-dramatizing. (Did her great-uncle hate anything so much as theater displacing life: all things that did not blend and disappear into his scheme of things, silent and reticent so that he, Mr. Halston, could occupy the dignified center of the world? How far, she almost cried in rage.) They reminded her of Mantegna's Christ, so lonely at his death table, His feet, His whole body jutting out of the canvas, kicking the spectator as if wishing violently to arouse him or her to the fact that death was not noble but base, not serene but convulsive, not promising but irrevocable, unredeemable: the glassy half-opened eyes, the skimpy two-week beard, the ulcerated feet, the breathless half-opened mouth, the clogged nostrils, the blood-clotted flanks, the matted hair soaked in dust and sweat, the terrifying sensation of the presence of the newly dead, of their swearing and bearing and walking and standing erect just a few hours before. Arroyo was right as he spoke of his father's death and the son's vigil over the remains: what if they suddenly sprang back and proved we were already dead (this is what she had known a moment before as she lay with Arroyo in the railroad car) and were doubling our time in another circumstance, another place, another time. Were all these bodies lying around the square carefully stretched out there like so many bleached dolls (pale as the haze Arroyo dreaded on the lowlands yet craved on the tops of mountains) simply the proof that they themselves—the old man and the young general, her errant father and her abiding mother, little Pedro and the moon-faced woman—were all bodies occupied by the dead, carcasses presently inhabited by people called Harriet Winslow, Tomás Arroyo, Ambrose Bierce . . . She stopped in a cold fright, as if naming someone, especially for the first time, was indeed a violation of his life: by saying this name, she immediately condemned the old man to death, she saw him now lying there among the corpses on the battlefield, wondering if Arroyo had killed him, or she in her imagination, or he himself in his own dark, labyrinthine desire; a name she had read on the covers of the books the old man carried with him, a name that was surely not his, because he did not want to be named and she respected his express desire, thus respecting the unexpressed ones as well: she was learning to take care of the unseen through what she saw, and of what she saw through what she could not see. These corpses had been animate a few hours before, and now she was seeing them ripped open by bayonets, their guts spilling out, their brains shot through by bullets, their chests punctured by shrapnel, their legs erupting in red volcanic holes of sulfuric powder, their buttocks caked with the last shit, their trousers wet with the last urine— the last seed, maybe, if they had died with the erections some men have when facing death. Ambrose Bierce was a dead name printed on the covers of two books the old man traveled with. She could not call him Cervantes, the author's name on the other book. So maybe calling him Bierce was just as farfetched. But this latter name gave her a chill: it was an invisible name, simply because the old man had no name; it was, already, a dead name. As dead as the corpses neatly laid out around the village square. Did *they* ever have names?

Who was there among the bodies she now saw tracing zigzags across that square whom she had now seen in feast and in mourning, as the wailing women set up shop in the corners and began their ritualistic metamorphoses of both life and death into gestures and words: who was there whom she knew among them? Was her own father there? Was the old gringo there? Was Arroyo's father there in the midst of the wailing and the rising dust and the dying embers of forgotten meals?

"My father was shot to death in Yucatan. The old fucker was determined to have a beautiful Indian girl in the hacienda of none other than don Olegario Molina, who was endlessly the governor of the province. Those were the days of the sisal boom. We all knew that noth-

ing made as much money as the maguey crop. Yucatan
was ruled by the divine caste—that's what they called
themselves, the fucking swine. My father was a big landowner up north, where we are now; desert and cattle and
a few vines here and there, and also agave plants and
good cotton crops. Cold nights, here in the desert, you
know. High up, thin air. Down there they say it's hot
and damp all year. A brittle crust of land, riverless. Deep
wells. Gray jungles, they say. I have not been there. They
say virgins used to be thrown into the wells. My father
was a guest and felt he had a right to the beautiful girl
he saw working in the hacienda. It happens all the time.

"He had her, they say, right on the eve of the Revolution. He was old then, but as much of a cock as ever.
Maybe because the land was all smelling of sulfur and
blood, he thought he was going to plunge into the pit
of hell soon and should hurry for his last big glorious
fuck. They say he had her in his own room and she
kicked the mosquito net down on them and he growled
with pleasure at this, feeling the moistness of her blood
staining the net as the flies and insects got caught in the
fabric falling like a light but strangling cloud upon them,
and the brass stands shivered, and the girl, too. Now
another man like me—her sweetheart, you know, her
promised one—was in charge of the keys of that hacienda, of winding the clock maybe, who knows? and he
saw her come out of my father's room and struck her in
the face with the keys, but she did not cry out, she said
he's in there—my father's in there, gringuita, again rubbing his ulcerated cock, rubbing it clean of blood, a
strong old man now with his penis eternally smeared
with blood, imagining he was fucking, in one virgin girl,
all the women of Mexico in their moon days, having

[194]

the moon as he had a woman, oh, the fucking bastard, how I hate him and how I wish I had been there when this young couple, a couple like me and . . . and . . . and . . . God damn it, not you, Miss Harriet, damn you, not like you, like another woman I never had, not like La Luna either, oh, damn it, that last girl my father ever had is like no woman I have ever had, oh, damn you, gringa, no one like that woman, I say damn you and damn La Luna and all the other women who do not resemble my own mother, who is the twin sister of the last woman my damned father ever had: they killed him right there in the bed, you know how? It is horrible: they stuck the keys of the hacienda into his mouth, all of them, made him swallow keys, gringa, until he choked and turned blue on metal, and then they dragged him out wrapped up in the mosquito netting and the sheets in the high hours of the night, when daybreak is never to be suspected. They put him into the laundry basket and waited until dawn, then they took him to the deep well, and he hung him there, hung him from his balls with a hook they use for the sisal bales, gringa, and he told her: I am going off to the Revolution, but you stay here and say nothing. You come and see him rot hanging from his balls right here where no one will know where he is. You don't know anything, remember. Just come and see him alone. Don't let anyone know. You will tell me when he has rotted and there is nothing left of him but his clean old bones. Then you can discover him and let him have a Christian burial.

"I come from the north. This unknown man, my father's killer, is from the south. The Revolution moves. We will meet somewhere. Maybe in the capital, in Mexico City. I will embrace him. He will come to see this land where my father was once powerful and feared. I will go down to see the land where he is a skeleton hanging in a well."

"You will also love the girl, and take her from your father's killer."

"Perhaps."

Then he took her once more and as she felt that rough and svelte body pounding so fiercely and so sweetly against her clitoris, knowingly stroking it with his own nervous and sleek body as he lasted inside her for an eternal moment, waiting for her to come, relying not only on his hard shaft but on this stroking, pounding, second heartbeat from his pubis on her clitoris, she knew that this was an instant and that she would never have it again, not because she could not have the sex again and again and again, but because she could have nothing else of Arroyo's. She came with an unbearable groan, a great animal moan she would have tolerated in no one, a sinful sigh of pleasure that was God-defying, duty-mocking (she would not have tolerated it in herself, a month ago), a scream of love that told the world that this was the only thing worth doing, worth having, worth knowing, nothing else in the world, nothing else but this instant between that other instant that gave us birth and that final instant that took our life away forever. Between these two moments, let me have only this moment, she prayed, and then violently wrenched herself from Arroyo's body with a gesture more fearful than castration, a gesture of boundless hatred for the man who offered her what she knew could never be, and knowing this, she found out that what he was giving her and could give her at any time was precisely what he could not give her: the translation of the plenitude of his body into the long, piecemeal, squandered, pedestrian voyage into the years. This exceptional instant was hers forever, but the source of the instant could never be. For the girl waiting for a corpse to rot hanging over a sacred well in Yucatan, it could be, or for a shoeless old man who refused city clothes, or a child-bearing woman called La Garduña, or a moon-faced woman who permitted her lover to take other women as she patiently waited outside the door—for a virtually idolatrous people on their knees moving toward a bloodied Christ swathed in velvet and crowned with thorns, or another murderous young man, Arroyo's double, marching with the Revolution from the south to meet Arroyo at the navel of this country that was like a brown body, the sum of its brown bodies, shaped like an empty cornucopia of hard skin and thirsty flesh and sweating thighs and scrawny arms— for them all, it could be, but never for her, it could never have a meaning, a prolongation, a continued presence in her own future, whatever that might be.

It was at that moment, in Arroyo's arms, that she hated Arroyo most for this: she had known this world and could never be part of it and he knew it, yet he gave it to her, let her taste it, but knew that nothing could keep them together forever, and maybe even laughed at her: Wouldn't you have been better off if you had never come here, gringuita? And she said no. If I had treated you with respect? And she said no. If I had sent you back immediately to the border escorted by my men? And she said no. If you stayed here with me forever and I left La Luna and you came with me to meet my unknown brother from Yucatan who murdered my father?

And she said no, no, no. (If we lived together and raised children and got married and grew old together, sí, gringuita?)

No.

"You're afraid a bullet will kill me any day?"

"No. I'm afraid of what you may kill."

"Ha, your gringo, you think?"

"And yourself, Arroyo. I fear what you might do to yourself."

"Believe me, gringa, I am not myself most of the time. I come rushing out, in swift movement, from all I have told you: my past is the wolf that pursues me over this desert. I have stopped here at the home that was my past. But it is no longer that. And now I know it. We must move on. The movement has not ceased."

"Have you disobeyed orders by staying here too long?"

"No. I am fighting. Those are my orders. But"—Arroyo laughed—"Pancho Villa hates anyone who thinks about going back home. It is like treason, almost. I have gambled heavily by taking the Miranda hacienda and remaining here."

He was going south, to Mexico City, to meet his brother who killed his father.

She was not.

"This cannot be," she said bitterly. "You are offering me what I can never be."

And this she never forgave Tomás Arroyo.

She would have liked, at the end, to reach out to touch the old man's bony, freckled hand, with its thick wedding ring, and tell him that she did what she did, not to avenge him, but to repay Arroyo for the wrong he did her: he knew she would never be what he had shown her she could be. Condemned to return home with the body of the old gringo, she had to show Arroyo that no one has the right to go home again.

And yet Harriet Winslow knew (she said so to the lost writer, stroking his hand covered with white hair) that she had not harmed Arroyo but given him a hero's victory: a young death. The old gringo, too, had won his own victory: he came to Mexico to die. Ah, old man, you did it. didn't you—you're the good-looking corpse you wanted to be. Ah, General Arroyo, you did it, didn't you—you died young, as you wanted to die. Ah, old man. Ah, young man.

 Now she sits alone and remembers.